Matt yanked open the door

Then froze as he came face-to-face with the woman who had haunted his dreams for three long months.

Camille stepped a little closer, leaned against the doorway, and her signature scent—lavender and brown sugar and sweet, ripe strawberries—wrapped itself around him. Still, he didn't say anything. Didn't touch her, though every instinct he had demanded that he grab onto her before she pulled another vanishing act.

"It's good seeing you, Camille. You look great. But I'm a little busy. So if you wouldn't mind—"

"I do mind."

"Excuse me?"

"I should be in Florence right now, combing museums with a glorious man named Stefano and eating pasta on the patio of a little trattoria."

"So, why aren't you?"

"Because I'm three months pregnant."

And just like that, his world imploded.

Dear Reader,

I've always been a sucker for stories where opposites attract because I believe the differences keep the sparks alive and the sparks are what make everyday living an adventure.

In *Beginning with Their Baby,* I bring back Matt Jenkins, the best friend and business partner of Reece, my hero in *From Friend to Father.* Matt is a stand-up guy. He plays by the rules and does the right thing. Camille Arraby is his polar opposite in every way—she's capricious, refuses to settle down and flits from one temporary job to another as she travels the world. She's so commitment-phobic that the idea of signing a six-month lease on an apartment makes her hyperventilate. Yet from the second I put these two in a room together, sparks flew!

Writing their story reminded me of my own marriage. My husband is an electrical engineer and I'm a writer. He's an introvert and I'm an extrovert. He's all about making a plan and I love to fly by the seat of my pants—and these are just the superficial differences. There are many more that go so deep that when we got married, no one thought it would last. Yet here we are three kids and fourteen years later, still going strong—and still striking sparks off each other.

I hope you enjoy reading *Beginning with Their Baby* as much as I enjoyed writing it. Please, visit me at www.tracywolff.com or on my blog, tracywolff.blogspot.com and let me know what you think.

Happy reading!

Tracy Wolff

Beginning with Their Baby
Tracy Wolff

HARLEQUIN®

TORONTO • NEW YORK • LONDON
AMSTERDAM • PARIS • SYDNEY • HAMBURG
STOCKHOLM • ATHENS • TOKYO • MILAN • MADRID
PRAGUE • WARSAW • BUDAPEST • AUCKLAND

Recycling programs
for this product may
not exist in your area.

ISBN-13: 978-0-373-71649-4

BEGINNING WITH THEIR BABY

Copyright © 2010 by Tracy L. Deebs-Elkenaney.

www.eHarlequin.com

Printed in U.S.A.

ABOUT THE AUTHOR

Tracy Wolff collects books, English degrees and lipsticks, and has been known to forget where—and sometimes who—she is when immersed in a great novel. At six she wrote her first short story—something with a rainbow and a prince—and at seven she forayed into the wonderful world of girls' lit with her first Judy Blume novel. By ten she'd read everything in the young adult and classics sections of her local bookstore, so in desperation her mom started her on romance novels. And from the first page of the first book, she knew she'd found her lifelong love. Now a writing professor at her local community college, Tracy is thrilled to be writing novels for Harlequin Superromance. She lives in Austin, Texas, with her husband and three young sons.

Books by Tracy Wolff

HARLEQUIN SUPERROMANCE
1529—A CHRISTMAS WEDDING
1568—FROM FRIEND TO FATHER
1607—THE CHRISTMAS PRESENT

Don't miss any of our special offers. Write to us at the following address for information on our newest releases.

Harlequin Reader Service
U.S.: 3010 Walden Ave., P.O. Box 1325, Buffalo, NY 14269
Canadian: P.O. Box 609, Fort Erie, Ont. L2A 5X3

For the Pitts, the best group of women I know.

Acknowledgments

Thank you to Wanda Ottewell, my wonderful and
intrepid editor, for always knowing what my books
need—even when I don't.

And to my fabulous agent, Emily Sylvan Kim,
who sticks by me no matter what.
You're the best!

PROLOGUE

"DO YOU HAVE TO GO?"

A twinge of uneasiness worked its way down Camille Arraby's spine at the words, though she continued to load her overnight bag. "My flight leaves in two hours—I've got to get to the airport."

"That's not what I meant and you know it." Matt Jenkins climbed off the rumpled bed where they'd just spent another incredible night, and walked toward her.

She watched him prowl across the room, his long, lean, nearly naked form a truly beautiful sight this early in the morning. His dark auburn hair had fallen over his eyes and his too-full lips were curved in the sexy grin she loved.

The twinge got a little more pronounced and for the first time that she could remember, Camille regretted the fact that she had to go. She wasn't nearly as ready to leave Austin—and Matt—as she'd expected to be.

But Brazil—and Carnaval—were in full swing and they wouldn't wait forever. Besides, it was better to walk away now, on a high note, than wait for things to sour as they inevitably would.

"So what *did* you mean?" she asked lightly, as he circled her waist with his hands and pulled her close.

"I was asking you to stay." He nuzzled her neck and she sighed, letting her head fall back as desire moved through her all over again.

"I can't."

His mouth moved lower, to the hollow of her throat, and she actually felt her knees tremble. "You can."

"Matt. You knew all along I was leaving today."

"I know."

"So what's the problem?" Her voice hitched as he flicked open the first two buttons of her shirt, ran his tongue over the curve of her breast.

"The problem is that when we made the deal, I didn't expect that I'd want you to stay."

"And now you do?"

He lifted his head so that his warm brown eyes met hers and Camille shuddered with unfulfilled desire. She'd never met a man like Matt, who could make her respond so effortlessly—and powerfully—to his lightest touch.

"Now I do." He stroked the back of his hand down her cheek. "Stay, Camille. Please. I've never felt like this before and I want to see where it goes."

"I've already given up my room and my job, already have my flights booked to Rio and then on to Italy."

"You can stay with me for a while—and getting another one of those temp jobs of yours can't be that difficult. You've been through three in the two months I've known you."

For one long second, Camille let his words sweep over her. Let herself imagine staying here with Matt indefinitely—spending hours and days and weeks together, in bed and out.

Doing all those wonderful things couples did when they were falling in love.

The images that flashed through her mind didn't send her running for the hills as they normally would have, and that—more than anything else could—had her taking a cautious step back.

Pulling free of Matt's embrace, she turned back to her bag. Rearranged the items in it, once, twice. Made sure her favorite brushes and palette were safe from shifting during travel as she struggled for the right words to say. But nothing came and silent minutes dragged by as Matt waited patiently for her answer, not pushing her but not backing down, either.

As she slid her makeup case to the bottom of the bag, Camille wanted nothing more than to run—as fast and as far as she could.

Wanted nothing more than to fling herself into Matt's arms and stay until this thing between them burned itself out.

But doing that was only asking for trouble, only asking for entanglements. Already Matt had sneaked through a crack in her defenses and taken up residence in an untouched spot in her heart. If she stayed, his presence inside her would grow until she was no longer complete without him. And that was something she would never, *could never,* allow.

When she finally looked up at him again, Camille made sure none of her doubts—none of her longing—showed on her face. "I can't stay, Matt. I was perfectly clear about the fact that I was leaving when we hooked up."

"I know. But plans can change."

"Not mine."

"Bull." This time when he grabbed her, his hands weren't quite as gentle as they had been. Somehow, the edginess was just as arousing as the care. "Your plans change all the time. They change with the wind, with your whims. Why can't you change them now? For me?"

"My plane tickets are nonrefundable." Her answer was flippant, but her heart was pounding hard and fast.

He cursed. "I'll pay for the stupid tickets. I'll pay for a hundred tickets if you'll stay for just a little while longer." His hands slid up her arms and neck until he was cupping her face. "Please, Camille."

"Matt." She shook her head, fought against the lump in her stomach that was growing with every word he said.

"Damn it, do you think this is easy for me? I'm not used to having to beg a woman to spend time with me."

Of course he wasn't used to begging—he was gorgeous and smart, and if not rich, certainly well-off from his partnership in one of the city's leading architectural firms. He was a prime catch—just one more reason she was determined to throw him back before he could do the same to her.

Before she broke her own rules and forgot why she couldn't settle down.

Before *she* was the one pleading with *him* to stay.

"I don't want this." The words came out sharp, stilted.

"So what *do* you want?"

"To see Carnaval. To dance in the plaza and run through the streets with the parades. To visit the art museums and hang glide through the hills. I want to stand on the beach at dawn and watch the tide roll in."

"Okay. All right." He closed his eyes, ran a hand over his face. "Give me a couple days, let me rearrange my schedule and I'll go with you. You'll still see plenty of Carnaval."

The twinge turned into a full-blown panic attack as she slung her bag over her shoulder. "Come on, Matt. It's been fun, but we both know it's time to move on— before things get messy and predictable."

"They don't have to—"

"Sure they do, sweets." With a sassy grin, Camille reached up and patted her soon-to-be ex-lover's cheek. "That's the way of relationships. Short and fun turns long and nasty, until both people wish they'd gotten out when the getting was good."

He clenched his jaw. "Do you really believe that?"

"I do. And so do you—at least you did two months ago, when we first met."

"That was different."

"Baby, it's always different." She started to say more, but a car horn sounded from the street in front of his house. "I've got to go. My cab's here."

"I thought I was taking you to the airport."

"It's still early—go back to bed." Standing on tiptoes, she brushed her lips against his once, twice. Then gasped as his mouth turned frenzied on hers.

He kissed her like no one ever had—hard and hot and with a desperation that nearly overwhelmed her.

That nearly had her dropping her bag and following him back into bed, where he was so sure they belonged.

That nearly had her saying to hell with Rio and Italy and the world—she was more than content to stay right here, in Austin, Texas.

But then the horn sounded again and she was pulling away. Smiling at him. Walking out the door and reminding herself, with every step, of all the reasons she was doing the right thing.

After all, there was a big, bright world out there, and in her thirty-two years she'd only managed to see about three-quarters of it. It was time—past time—to get started visiting the last quarter.

CHAPTER ONE

MATT SMILED AS HE SLID his homemade lasagna onto the table, alongside the crusty loaf of garlic bread and fancy tossed salad that were already there.

"Would you like some wine?" He dropped the oven mitts and reached for the bottle of red he'd picked out to go with the meal. Like his dinner companion, it was rich and voluptuous and very easy on the tongue.

"I would love some." Ariane smiled as she held up her glass.

He filled it to the halfway mark, then did the same for his own before settling into his seat. It had been a long time since he'd cooked dinner for a woman, but he'd planned tonight carefully. Ariane was the first woman he'd been interested in since Camille, and after four dates, he was pretty sure she was amenable to his anticipated ending for the evening.

And if he wasn't nearly as excited as he should be about that ending, then he needed to get over it. Camille was gone, and after spending the first few weeks leaving messages on her cell phone and several more weeks moping around, he'd finally figured out that she wasn't coming back.

Even then, after he'd accepted that Camille was out of his life for good, it had taken him a while to move on. But he'd finally done it. He'd found a woman who was interested in him—as both a person *and* a good time. And now he was convinced this was for the best. His time with Camille, while lovely, had been an aberration, a step outside his comfort zone into chaos and insanity.

It had been a bad move and one he had no desire to repeat. All he'd gotten from trying something different was a bruised heart, a battered ego and a headache the size of Texas.

No, it was better all around if he stuck to his regular, controlled agenda from now on. And tonight, that agenda included taking his relationship with Ariane to the next step.

"This was so sweet, Matt. It's been a long time since a man cooked me dinner."

"It's been a long time since I've cooked a woman dinner. I hope I haven't lost my touch."

"I'm sure it will be delicious." She smiled warmly at him.

As he dished up the lasagna, he asked, "How's that case going? The one that was giving you such trouble?"

"It's an absolute disaster. I'm defending this corporation and it's obvious to everyone but them that they're guilty as hell of violating state and federal sexual harassment laws. I start presenting my case on Monday and I can only hope I can pull some magic out of my hat to confuse the jury about what was really going on in that factory."

A curl of unease started in Matt's belly at her words, but he ignored it. It was her job to defend corporations against lawsuits like this, he reminded himself. Of course she would do whatever she could do help her client win—even if they were guilty.

"Mmm, this is wonderful."

"Thanks."

"So how about you? How's that design going?"

"I finished it—and it is brilliant, if I do say so myself." He grinned over his glass of wine. "The clients are flying in tomorrow to see it, so I'll know for sure then. But Reece thinks we've knocked it out of the park."

"That's fabulous." She took another bite. "And really, so is this lasagna. How did you learn to cook like this?"

"I grew up with three sisters and my mom always believed that I should learn whatever the girls learned, and vice versa. So when she taught them to cook a few recipes, she made sure I was in the kitchen right along with them—even if I would have preferred to be playing football or basketball."

"I can just see you—a cute little boy with big eyes peering into his mother's spaghetti-sauce pot."

He snorted. "More like a surly preteen whining about how I'd never need to know how to cook because when I grew up I was going to live on pizza and hamburgers."

"Well, I'm glad your mother didn't listen."

Their eyes met across the table. "So am I."

Her smile turned soft, intimate. It was one of the things that had attracted him to her when they'd met a few weeks before—that and her softly rounded curves. Camille had been all angles and mile-long legs and it was nice to hold on to a woman who wasn't so...sharp.

Add in Ariane's sense of order and dedication to the University of Texas's football team—she was a Longhorn, too—and he'd been sold.

"You know, Matt, I really like you."

"I like you, too, Ariane." His heart beat a little faster in anticipation. "Very much."

She pushed her plate away. "Then maybe we should skip dessert…"

There they were, the words he'd been waiting to hear for weeks. He'd expected his body to respond right away, but now that she'd extended the invitation, he wasn't nearly as interested as he'd expected to be. Still, she was a beautiful, intelligent woman and would make a great girlfriend.

Without giving himself any more time to think, Matt slid his chair back and reached for her plate. "And what would you like to do in lieu of dessert?" he asked, making sure to keep his voice low and teasing.

She stood, as well. "Oh, I'm sure we can think of something."

He reached for her hand, but a knock at his front door stopped him before he could pull her against him. "Why don't you go into the family room? I'll join you as soon as I answer that."

"Don't be long."

"Believe me, I won't be." He strode to the door, pulled it open with a yank. Then froze as he came face-to-face with the woman who had haunted his dreams for nearly three long months.

For a minute, the whole world stood still while he soaked in the vision that was Camille. Her black hair was shorter and sassier than it had been when she'd left, but everything else was the same.

The flawless expanse of golden skin her halter dress showed off.

The wicked curve of her sexily uneven mouth.

The killer legs that had had him waking up hard and sweaty and frustrated as hell for weeks after she'd left.

She'd come back, he told himself as his traitorous body responded to her proximity. Even after everything she'd said, after ignoring his text messages and phone calls for months, she'd come back.

How pathetic did it make him that he was excited by that fact?

She stepped a little closer, leaned against the doorway, and her signature scent—lavender and brown sugar and sweet, ripe strawberries—wrapped itself around him. He went from semiaroused to rock hard in an instant.

Still, he didn't say anything. Didn't touch her, though every instinct he had demanded that he grab on to her before she pulled another vanishing act.

The thought had the same effect as a freezing shower, and the connection between them shattered. He couldn't hold her tightly enough to keep her from leaving again—she was like the wind, blowing from one place to another with little thought to the destruction she left in her path.

He wasn't going to be part of the fallout again.

"What are you doing here, Camille?" he demanded, forcing a calm into his voice that he was far from feeling. But she was an expert at power games and there was no way in hell he was revealing a weakness. Not when she was so good at drawing first blood.

"I was in the neighborhood." Even the slow, honeyed drawl was the same. "Thought I'd drop by."

"Long walk from Italy."

She shrugged, unconcerned. "Yeah, well, Florence is overrated."

"Really?"

"No. But you know me. I get bored if I stay in one place too long."

"I remember." He kept his voice cool, made sure none of the confusion—or desire—he was feeling leaked through.

"Can I come in?"

"Now's not really a good time."

Uncertainty flashed across her face—was there and gone so quickly that he told himself he'd imagined it. "It won't take long. I just wanted to talk for a few minutes."

"Talk?" This time he let her see his skepticism—and a little bit of the anger he thought had dissipated in the weeks since she'd walked out. "Since when do you want to talk about anything? I thought action was more your thing."

As soon as the words were out, he wanted to call them back. Her smile had turned predatory, those amethyst-colored eyes running over him from head to toe. It was as if she was cataloging each one of his flaws and weaknesses, and he'd never felt more vulnerable.

"Bitter much?"

"I wouldn't call it bitter."

"No? Then what *would* you call it?"

"Smart." He grabbed the edge of the door, made as if to close it. "Now, if you will excuse me—"

"I really do need to talk to you."

"Yeah, well, I really needed to talk to you all those times I called you." Shit. He *did* sound bitter.

She sighed heavily, as if he was just too high mainte-nance for her. It was like setting a match to dry kindling and all the emotions that had been seething in him for the past few months came roaring out.

"Look, Camille, I don't know what kind of game you're playing, but count me out."

"I thought you liked games—at least, that's what you told me the night we met."

"I did—until you kept changing the rules without warning."

"I wasn't the one who changed the rules, sweets. You were."

He started to snap back, but how could he when she was right? She'd told him up front that she was only in town for a few weeks, that the thing between them couldn't go anywhere. He was the one who hadn't listened.

He was the one who'd gotten burned.

But at least he'd learned his lesson—he was done playing with fire.

"I'm tired, Camille, and I have company. Either say what you came here to say or leave—I really don't care. But I don't have the time or the inclination to stand out here all night shooting the breeze. I'm letting bugs in."

Her smile drooped a little at the edges, and she didn't answer for long seconds. Guilt slinked through him. Maybe he'd been too harsh. He could have said things more nicely, could have—

No! Damn it, no. She was the one who had walked out on him. The one who had come back here after ig-noring all his attempts to reach out to her in the hopes of picking up where they'd left off. And now, just when he'd started to move on, here she was. So why exactly should he make it easy for her?

Why should he have anything to do with her at all?

"Matt?" Ariane's voice drifted down the hall. "Can you bring my wine when you come in?"

"Aah." The hint of vulnerability was long gone, replaced by the party-girl mask he'd learned to hate during their brief affair. "You've got *that* kind of company."

He felt himself flush at her words, at the look in her eyes. But he didn't have anything to feel sheepish about, he reminded himself. She was the one who'd broken things off.

"Sure, Ariane." He raised his voice a little, so Ariane could hear him. "I'll be there in a minute." Then turned back to his most recent ex-lover.

"It was good seeing you, Camille. You look great. But, as you can see, I'm a little busy. So if you wouldn't mind heading out—"

"I do mind."

"Excuse me?"

"I should be in Florence right now, combing museums with a glorious man named Stefano and eating pasta on the patio of a little trattoria."

Who the hell was Stefano? Matt bit back the instinctive spurt of jealousy that flared. It wasn't his business what she did—or who she did it with. She'd made that abundantly clear when she'd walked out on him.

"So why aren't you?"

"Because I'm three months pregnant."

And just like that, his world imploded.

OH, GOD, HAD SHE REALLY just blurted it out like that? No finesse, no work-up? Just *I'm pregnant,* with *you're the father* strongly implied?

No wonder Matt looked like he'd fall over if she breathed too hard.

She'd planned on breaking it to him much more calmly. Had figured he'd invite her in for a cup of coffee and she could work her way around to it. But he hadn't invited her in, hadn't wanted anything to do with her.

His reaction had hurt her, made her angry—and careless. Of course, now that it was too late, she would do anything to take back her hasty words. Matt hadn't deserved to find out about his impending fatherhood so callously.

"Three months?" he finally asked, his voice low and hoarse.

"Yes."

"As in twelve weeks?"

"Yes."

"As in…"

"Yes. I got pregnant that last week in Austin." To his credit, he didn't ask if she was sure. Of course, that could be more from the shock than from any consideration for her. But somehow, she doubted it.

"I know this isn't what you were expecting," she began nervously. "And I'm sorry to spring it on you—believe me, when I first found out I didn't look any better than you do. And I thought about ending it—a baby doesn't exactly fit into my lifestyle—but when it got to be crunch time, I just couldn't do it. Maybe that's not fair to you, I don't know. All I know is that I'm having this baby and I figure you have the right to know about it."

"Get rid of it?"

She thought that sounded like a question, but she wasn't sure. Maybe it had been an order. Taking a deep breath, Camille flipped her hair out of her face—she wanted to make sure she had a good look at his face when they discussed this—and said, "I can't. I know it would make things easier and maybe it's the best decision. But I just…can't."

"That wasn't a suggestion. I was trying to decipher what you—" He swore, ran an unsteady hand over his face. "I wasn't prepared for this, Camille."

"Neither was I. Believe me. When I started throwing up in Florence I was sure I'd caught a bug—and not one of the nine-months variety."

"Matt? Are you coming?" Once again, the female voice floated down the hallway and Camille was glad to realize she didn't feel quite so sucker punched this second time. Not that she had any right to complain—and she wasn't. But still, knowing Matt was with another woman was…disconcerting.

He swore again, a little more loudly. "Uh, yeah, Ariane. Give me a minute."

He looked so flustered that she couldn't help feeling contrite. Blurting it out like that had been a ridiculous thing to do, especially when Matt was obviously on a date. But she'd given herself a pep talk all the way over here and she hadn't been able to hold the words in any longer. She'd wanted to say them—to somebody.

Saying them made the baby real, certainly more real than it had been since she'd stood in the middle of her small Italian flat and tried to decipher the pregnancy test directions, which had been written in Italian.

Despite the language barrier, the fact that the little window had turned blue had left her with little doubt as to whether or not she was pregnant. As she'd stared at the small, slender wand she'd been scared. Shocked. And more than a little horrified. But as the minutes and hours and finally days passed, she'd managed to wrap her mind around the concept of being pregnant. The baby was still a mystery—one she had no idea what to do with—but she figured she had six months to learn. After all, she had an entire pregnancy to get through before she had to worry about an actual baby. Thank God.

"Look, I'm sorry to just barge in here like this. I guess I didn't think this thing through as well as I could have. I'll come back later, when you're not…entertaining."

She started to turn away, but his hand snaked out and grabbed her wrist. "You're not getting off that easily."

"What does that mean?" She felt her own back go up.

"It means, you can't just breeze in here and drop a bombshell like that and then turn around and walk back out."

"I know that," she snarled, trying to extricate herself from his painless but nevertheless firm grip. "But I figured you had other things to do right now. Call me on my cell when—"

"Yeah, because that works so well." He thrust his free hand through his thick fall of auburn hair. "I'm not letting you out of here until we settle some things—"

"Matt?"

At the interruption, Camille glanced over Matt's shoulder at his date. Her stomach sank at the first glimpse of the tiny but voluptuous blond woman. Exquisitely dressed and exceptionally beautiful, she was everything Camille wasn't. Suddenly she felt like the tall, ungainly elephant in the room, even though she was still a couple of months from showing.

But still, how could she compete with Ariane? If this was Matt's regular type, then Camille—with her normal attire of jeans and tank tops and paint-splattered skin—didn't stand a chance.

The thought brought her up cold, had her backing out the front door without even bothering to glance behind her to see where she was going.

Not that she wanted a chance with Matt, she assured herself viciously as she teetered on the edge of the first step. He wasn't her usual type any more than she was his. And she didn't want to get tied down to any one man anyway. That was just asking for trouble.

Nothing had changed since she'd left here twelve weeks before. It just felt like everything had.

"Camille, look out!" Matt had followed her out onto the porch and now he reached for her a second time, stopping her from falling down the stairs. She wondered if she should feel grateful that he'd saved her from looking ridiculous as well as stupid. One thing was for certain—she was making one hell of a second impression.

Taking a deep breath, she met Matt's warm, brown eyes for the third time that night. "Thanks. Another guy would have let me fall—at least then all your problems would be over."

She watched as his face turned from concerned to angry, the little laugh lines at the corners of his eyes getting deeper as he frowned. "That's an awful thing to say. I would never—"

"I know, I know." She backed down the steps, this time keeping a hand on the railing and glancing behind her to make sure she didn't stumble again. "That's what I was trying to say. Not all guys are like you.

"Do you still have my cell number? If not, I can call you tomorrow sometime and we can get together for coffee and—" she darted a look at the petite blonde, who was looking more and more confused—and annoyed—by the minute "—talk about the project," she improvised wildly, not wanting to ruin his evening any more than she already had. "I'm sorry for bothering you at home. This can definitely wait for a better time. I'll just—"

"Camille, stop."

Matt's voice rang out and she froze, shocked at how quickly he'd gone from easygoing to authoritative.

"We need to talk."

She swallowed nervously, wondered how on earth she'd managed to get herself into this predicament. "I know and we will. Later." She was almost at her car, almost free.

"I know running is your favored modus operandi, but that's not going to work with this. I want—"

"Matt, what's going on here?" Ariane spoke for the first time since coming down the hall. Matt turned to her and it was all the distraction Camille needed. Her keys were already in her hand—she realized dazedly she'd never even put them away—and she dived toward her rental car like a desert wanderer toward an oasis.

Running away might be the coward's way out, but right now she preferred to consider it a strategic retreat. There was no way she could talk to Matt about the baby with the perfect Ariane anywhere in the picture.

After fumbling the keys into the ignition, she pulled away from the curb. The last thing she saw as she drove away was Matt standing on the sidewalk, mouth drawn and narrowed as he watched her leave. Again.

CHAPTER TWO

AN HOUR LATER, CAMILLE SAT on her anonymous motel bed eating Cherry Garcia ice cream right out of the container—and not being the least bit dainty about it.

Now that she was away from Matt and his date, she felt ridiculous for running. Even more ridiculous for blurting things out the way she had. She, who had been known for her clear head and ballsy demeanor for most of her adult life, had totally choked. And now they were both paying the price for it.

Still, what had she been thinking just showing up at Matt's house like that? He was a great guy, with the typical sex drive of a thirty-five-year-old male. Was it any wonder, then, that he had a girlfriend? It had been twelve weeks since she'd walked away from him. What had she expected—that he'd wait around and pine for her forever?

She nearly laughed at the thought, the image of the gorgeous Ariane emblazoned forever in her brain. Camille had no delusions about her own attractiveness—she knew she was far from beautiful. *Striking* was how most people described her. Not easy to forget. Through the years she'd learned to play to her strengths, emphasizing her unusual coloring and irregular features instead of playing them down.

And usually she was okay with it. She shook her head, took another big mouthful of ice cream. Who was she kidding? She'd always been okay with it—right up until she'd come face-to-face with the woman who'd replaced her in Matt's affections. Which was absurd. Just because he was the father of her baby didn't mean he was going to be anything more to her.

She didn't *want* him to be anything more.

When her phone rang, she almost ignored it. After all, Matt was probably still tied up with the blonde wonder and she wasn't exactly in the mood to talk to anyone else. But curiosity had her digging in her pocket for her cell.

Matt's name scrolled across the small screen and her hands grew damp. She wasn't ready for this, hadn't recovered from the embarrassment of her less than graceful retreat. Besides, she'd figured he had more exciting plans than talking to her tonight. She hadn't expected a call until sometime tomorrow.

Nerves on red alert, she answered with a soft "Hello."

"Where are you?"

"I'm at my motel."

"I figured that—which one?"

"Why?"

"Why do you think?" He sounded angry and frustrated and more than a little out of sorts. "I'm coming over."

"It can wait until tomorrow—"

"Keep dreaming, Camille. And tell me where you are."

She rattled off the name of the motel, along with its cross streets, her heart pounding like a rock song.

"What room?"

"Two-thirteen."

"I'll be there in fifteen minutes. Don't go any-where."

He clicked off and she was left staring at a dead phone. And wishing that the next hour was already over. Anything was better than the sick curl of antici-pation working its way through her pregnancy-churned stomach.

MATT POUNDED UP THE STAIRS that led to Camille's motel room, his heart in his throat and his blood pres-sure through the roof.

Pregnant. Camille was *pregnant.* With *his* child.

Just the thought boggled the brain.

He'd used a condom, hadn't he? Every time? Then how was she— He yanked his thoughts back to the present, but it wasn't easy. Nothing had been from the moment he'd opened his door and seen Camille standing there.

He didn't even know what he'd said to get rid of Ariane. After Camille had driven away, he'd stood on the sidewalk looking after her car for God only knew how long as he tried to assimilate her words. He hadn't succeeded.

Finally, a less than happy Ariane had come outside looking for him. She'd wanted to pick the date up where they'd left off, before Camille's interruption, but he'd been too shocked to do more than utter the most banal of excuses as he showed her the door.

She hadn't been impressed, but he hadn't cared. He still didn't care, as all his thoughts and energy were currently wrapped up in Camille's bombshell.

Pregnant.

Camille was pregnant.

He kept hoping that repeating the words would make them seem more real—and him less clueless. But the truth was he didn't even know where to start trying to figure this mess out.

When he got to room 213, he pounded on the door hard enough to let Camille know he wasn't taking no for an answer. How she'd thought he'd want to wait until tomorrow to talk to her, he'd never know. But then again, he'd never been able to figure out what was going on in Camille's brain. Case in point—the whole debacle three months ago when he'd begged her to stay. And she'd batted him away as if he were a pesky gnat.

Then Camille's door was swinging open and any and all confused thoughts he'd been able to form between his house and here completely flew out of his head. Not that it was anything new—his first glimpse of her, even when they'd been dating, had always done that to him.

There was just something about her that knocked him stupid.

Trying to buy himself a few seconds, he glanced at the half-eaten container of ice cream in her hand, cataloged the lines of strain around her eyes and mouth.

"You look tired," he finally said.

"I'm jet-lagged. I just got in from Italy today."

"How long have you known?"

"About the baby?"

He nodded.

"Five days."

Something cold melted in his chest. She'd just found out she was pregnant and had come straight back to Austin to tell him about the baby. At least she hadn't been keeping it from him.

At least she'd been willing to trust him that much.

"Okay." He glanced behind her, to her empty motel room. The television murmured quietly in the background. "Can I come in?"

"Yeah, sure." She turned away, leaving him to follow.

When she sank onto the bed, he had a moment's indecision. Should he sit next to her? Stand? For a man who always knew where he was going and what he was doing, it was a less than impressive feeling.

He glanced around. It was a typical motel room—a bed, a table and chair, a dresser. He crossed the worn beige carpet, pulled out the chair and sat down. He didn't trust himself to get too close to her—the room smelled like her and he could feel his body responding, despite the numerous warnings he'd given himself on the way over.

Judging from the look on Camille's face, he figured anything she viewed as an advance on his part would be met with solid resistance. Not to mention a kick in the ass.

Not that he wanted to put the moves on her, he assured himself and his unruly erection. He'd given up on that stupidity a few weeks before, when he'd finally figured out that she wasn't going to come back. He'd resigned himself, then, to the fact that he would never be with her again.

Too bad his body didn't feel the same way.

Silence seethed between them. With each second that passed he could see Camille getting more agitated, her eyes darting between him, the TV and the Ben & Jerry's container in a pattern that would have been funny if he wasn't so damned strung out himself.

Maybe he should have mercy on her—she looked as shell-shocked as he felt. But as he watched her, Matt realized he was still too raw to feel very merciful. Her abandonment had really done a number on him—more so than he'd ever expected.

So, instead of breaking the uncomfortable quiet, he just watched and waited. Finally, when her spoon scraped the bottom of the ice cream container—and she had nothing else to hold her attention—she murmured softly, "I'm sorry. I didn't mean to ruin your date."

Who was this woman and what had she done with the Camille he'd known? That Camille had never apologized once in the time they were together. So what had changed?

The difference made him uncomfortable, as if the ground beneath him was shifting with each step he took. Because of it, his voice was harsher than he'd intended when he asked, "You think my date was more important than talking to the mother of my child? What the hell do you think of me?"

"I didn't mean that." She shoved up from the bed, then tossed the empty ice cream container in the trash before crossing to him. There was a shadow of anger in her own eyes and he couldn't help being relieved. This was the Camille he knew—fiery and strong. He preferred her to the cold, fragile woman who'd opened the motel-room door.

"So what did you mean?"

"I know this is a shock—and my timing couldn't have been worse."

"It's no big deal. Ariane understood."

"Good."

The silence was back, yawning between them like an underground cavern waiting to be explored. This time, he was the first to break it.

"So what are you going to do?"

"I'm going to keep it."

"You said that earlier. I meant, what are you going to do when the baby comes?"

"I don't know. I'm still trying to wrap my head around the idea that there *is* a baby."

He glanced at her still-flat stomach, knowing exactly what she meant. He felt like he'd been pulled up short, run over by a steamroller. Pulled into a swirling abyss of emotions and decisions he was in no way ready for.

"I want to help." The words came out stilted, cool, and she stiffened in response.

"Look, I didn't come here to hit you up for money."

"Still, I want to help. And I don't just mean financially. That's my kid, too."

"Well, that wasn't the reaction I'd anticipated." The careless, mocking tone he knew so well was back, and he couldn't help being relieved. He knew how to deal with this Camille.

"So what did you anticipate? You fly halfway around the world and show up on my doorstep with no warning—you must have been expecting something."

"You didn't even ask me if the baby was yours."

His stomach churned acid at her words, until all he could think of was Camille in the arms of another man.

Other men. How many had there been since she'd left him, anyway? He shoved the uncomfortable images away—regret wouldn't change anything.

"I figured if you made the effort to tell me, you had to be pretty sure…"

"You're the father."

He released the breath he hadn't known he was holding. "All right, then. So what do we do now?"

"What do you mean?"

"Have you seen a doctor? Figured out where you want to live? Thought about getting a job? You don't have to work right now, if you don't want to. I make enough money to—"

"Whoa, Matt." It was the first time she'd said his name since she'd come back, and warmth curled through him. At least until her next words hit him. "I've barely begun to think things through. I came back because I figured I owed it to you to tell you about the baby face-to-face. But nothing says I'm going to stay here."

"Excuse me?"

"Austin isn't exactly my dream spot, you know." She glanced around the generic motel room. "I never planned to settle here."

"But my business is here. My life is here."

"That doesn't mean mine has to be."

Ice skated down his spine. "What are you saying, Camille? That you don't want me to be a part of this baby's life?"

"Are you saying you really *want* to be a part of its life?" She looked him up and down skeptically. "You don't exactly come across as a family man."

Her words came at him from left field. Sure, when they'd been together, he hadn't talked about wanting to get married and have a family. He hadn't wanted to spook her. But he'd always anticipated having a wife and kids someday—just because his parents' marriage hadn't worked out didn't mean he didn't believe in the institution.

The thought gave him pause, made him wonder if this thing with Camille would ruin all his plans for the future. He'd always planned to do things the normal way—wife first, then kids. Having a kid first—with a woman who had no feelings for him and no plans to stick around—hadn't been part of the agenda.

Would a woman like Ariane—smart, savvy, driven—accept his ties to another woman, accept the fact that he'd had a child out of wedlock? Or would his lack of formal relationship with Camille make her suspicious about his ability to commit?

With a sigh, he let the worries go—things were what they were and there was nothing he could do but to make new plans, plans that included his baby and its commitment-phobic mother.

"I find it hard to believe that *you* think you can criticize *me* on *my* lifestyle. When you can't even hold a job for more than a month at a time."

"I choose not to hold a job. There's a huge difference."

"Yeah—and the distinction's not a particularly flattering one to you."

"Oh, I don't know," she drawled. "I think footloose and fancy-free is a lot better than buttoned-up and bitter as hell."

"For the second time, I am *not* bitter."

"Now, there's a good defense." Her eyes mocked him even more than her words. "Denial's not just a river in Egypt, Matt."

"Babies have a way of tying you down, Camille. They need things like security and stability."

She clenched her hands into fists, and he stared at her long artist's fingers, fascinated. They still bore traces of blue and green paint, as if she'd finished a painting and caught a plane to America all in the same hour.

Of course, she might have done just that—it was her way. Attacking her on it was going to get them nowhere.

"Look, Camille, it's my turn to apologize. This whole baby thing came out of nowhere and it's made me a little punchy." He pushed out of the chair, strode over to where she was. "I can't imagine what it's done to you."

"It's freaked me out," she admitted candidly. "Turned my whole life upside down—and the kid isn't even here yet."

"That's kind of what I figured—and I'm not making this any easier for you." He settled himself next to her on the bed, rested a soft hand on her knee. A jolt of electricity ripped between them, but he worked to ignore it. Chemistry—or a lack thereof—had never been their problem.

Too bad he couldn't say the same thing about communication.

"Look, nothing has to be decided now. Right? So we can just take things slowly, see how they work out."

"How do you think they're going to work out?"

"I don't know, but I'm sure we'll think of something."

She didn't answer, just stared at him for so long that he began to feel like a bug under a microscope—and a dead one, at that.

Just when his nerves were at the breaking point, she whispered, "Okay."

Relief swept through him, though he didn't know why. This baby was a complication he didn't need. Yet the idea of her taking off again, of never seeing the baby he'd helped create, left him cold.

Clearing away the sudden lump in his throat, he asked, "Have you seen a doctor yet?"

"I figured I'd do that here."

"Do you have anyone in mind?"

She shook her head and he started to relax. This is what he was good at. Planning. Thinking things out. Getting things done. If she'd let him, he'd take care of everything. "I'll figure something out. My friend Reece's wife had a baby just a few weeks ago—maybe she knows someone."

"Same old Matt, taking care of anyone who will let him."

He forced himself not to take offense. "You're not anyone. You're the mother of my child."

"Matt, I didn't tell you about the baby because I wanted to guilt you into anything. I don't work that way."

"I realize that." He studied her, with her wild black curls and bottomless gypsy eyes. He did know it— that was the kicker. But that didn't mean he didn't feel responsible.

Hell, he *was* responsible.

"I just thought—" She blew out a breath, let her hand with its multicolored fingers rest on his. "I figured you should know."

"Well." He forced a smile. "Now I know."

"Now you know."

He reached into his pocket, pulled out his cell phone.

"What are you doing?"

"Texting Reece for the name and number of Sarah's doctor. I want to get you in to see someone as soon as possible."

"Why do tomorrow what you can do today, huh, Matt?"

He looked up from the message he was composing. "Why do today what you can put off until tomorrow, huh, Camille?"

She smiled at him, the first real smile he'd seen from her since she'd walked out his door all those weeks before. And just that easily, the knot in his stomach dissolved.

Everything was going to be fine. He'd get Camille to a doctor, get her set up in an apartment that had enough room—and light—for her to paint. After he'd checked with the doctor, of course, and made sure the fumes weren't bad for the baby.

He'd take care of everything—like he always did. After all, how hard could caring for one pregnant woman be?

CHAPTER THREE

CAMILLE JERKED INTO a sitting position, her foggy brain struggling to figure out what had woken her when it felt like she had just drifted to sleep. After rubbing the sleep out of her eyes, she glanced down at the clock on her bedside table and realized that she had only gotten two hours of sleep.

With a groan, she sank back under the covers and pulled her pillow over her ears—anything to get the incessant ringing to stop. A few moments later it did stop and she eased the pillow onto the bed beside her—only to scramble for it once the noise started up again.

What on earth was making—the motel phone. She squinted at the offending object, taking in the red message light blinking maniacally at the same time she reached the conclusion that her caller wasn't going to just hang up and try again later. Besides, she'd been in town less than a day—only one person knew to call her here and he wasn't known for his willingness to give up.

Fumbling for the phone, she dropped the receiver— twice—before managing to get it to her ear. "Hello."

"It's about time." Matt's voice came through the line, smooth and sexy and oh-so-efficient. It was more than enough to put her teeth on edge. "I was beginning to think you'd drowned in the shower."

"I was asleep."

"Well, get up. It's nearly ten and we have an eleven o'clock appointment with an obstetrician."

"What?" She struggled into a sitting position. "I told you I was pregnant twelve hours ago and you already have a doctor's appointment?"

"You're three months along—you need to be seen."

"Yes, but—"

"I'll be there in fifteen minutes. We can talk in the car. The doctor's office is across town and we need to get there early to fill out paperwork."

He hung up before she could say another word. Camille slid the receiver back into its cradle and then flopped back onto the bed. Since when had Matt turned into a general marshalling his troops for battle—and how had she been enlisted as one of those troops anyway?

As she stared at the ceiling, she couldn't figure out if she should be angry at his presumptuousness—and at the orders he'd barked at her—or just grateful that he'd handled the details of finding a doctor for her. At three months along, she knew she needed to be checked over—and soon—and she hadn't been relishing the thought of combing the yellow pages for a doctor. Still, it rankled that Matt hadn't even asked for her input....

Deciding to go along with his plans for now—she'd never been one to cut her nose off to spite her face—Camille threw back the covers and climbed out of bed. She stumbled to the bathroom, where a quick glance in the mirror showed she looked as bad as she felt. Maybe even worse.

The day was off to a fantastic start.

One quick shower, manic tooth brushing and hit-and-miss application of lip gloss and mascara later, she was feeling almost human. At least, until the knock on her door had her jumping in surprise and knocking her shin against the motel room's sharp-cornered dresser.

Her eyes darted to the clock. Had it really been fifteen minutes—yes, it had. Fourteen, to be exact. Not that she was surprised. In the time they'd been together, Matt had never once been late. As she was always running fifteen minutes behind, she'd admired that about him…then.

Slipping into her robe, she yanked open the door with a snarl. "How'd you get an OB appointment on such short notice?"

"He's a friend of mine. I knew him when I was at grad school." His eyes swept over her from head to toe and his mouth tightened. "He did me a favor, which is why I don't want to be late. Go get dressed."

"If you'd given me more warning—"

"I've been calling, off and on, since I got off the phone with him at 8:30. It's not my fault you sleep like the dead."

"I'm jet-lagged." She tossed the comment flippantly over her shoulder as she yanked a pair of jeans and a tank top out of the suitcase she had yet to unpack. No need for him to know that she'd spent the night staring at the television while thoughts of the future spun through her mind like a Tilt-A-Whirl at high speed.

"I know. And the articles I read last night said that pregnant women are always exhausted in the first few months—we'll go to the doctor and then I'll bring you back here to sleep."

"Why, thank you, *Daddy*. I really appreciate it." She sauntered into the bathroom, closed the door with a snap.

"Don't go there," he called through the door. "I'm not trying to order you around—I just want to make sure you and the baby are okay."

His concern warmed her, even as it made her heart hiccup a little in her chest. She'd been prepared for anger, annoyance, dismay—but his concern was unexpected. Not to mention disconcerting. She got dressed quickly, then took a couple of minutes to primp in the mirror— not because she thought she could do anything about the too-thin face with the dark circles that stared back at her, but because she didn't want Matt to think he could rush her. It set a bad precedent.

Only when her heartbeat was back to normal and she'd drawn her emotional armor around herself did she head back into the bedroom. "There better be coffee in that cup and it better be for me."

"It is." He held the large white-and-green cup out to her. "It's decaf. The Web sites said that caffeine—"

"Is bad for the baby. I get it." She took a sip of the fragrant brew and figured it was a sign of her willingness to play nice that she didn't whimper at the lack of kick.

"Are you ready to go?"

"Ready as I'll ever be." She hunted around for sandals, found them in a tangle under the desk. "We need to stop at a bank, though. I need money."

"Don't worry about it." He held the door open for her, waiting as she preceded him through.

"Matt."

"No charge for the first appointment—I told you he was a friend of mine."

"What happened to Sarah's obstetrician?"

"He retired. But Rick's a better bet, anyway. He's the best at what he does—even if his practice is on the other side of town."

"And he's really willing to see me for free?"

"Yes. I swear."

She turned and studied him suspiciously, but he seemed sincere. "Fine." Her reply was less than gracious, but she wasn't sure what to do with this man who took care of everything for her. She was used to taking care of herself and wasn't sure how to feel now that Matt was taking over.

When they got to his car, Matt held her door open for her—a habit she remembered from when they'd been together. How had she managed to get herself hooked up with one of the last gentlemen on the planet? It boggled the mind, so she let it go—it was far too early to contemplate issues of that weight, especially when the benign dictator next to her was denying her caffeine.

Right before he pulled into traffic, Matt reached behind him and handed her a brown paper bag. She opened it and didn't even bother to try and stifle her laugh.

"Trying to fatten me up?"

"I didn't know what you'd be in the mood for. Besides, pregnant women need calcium and vitamins and—"

She clapped a hand over his mouth with a playful grin. "I get it. You spent the night reading every prenatal Web site you could find."

He started to talk, but her hand was still over his lips. The motion of his jaw as he tried to speak had his lips brushing against her palm, and little shivers shot down her back at the sensation. She jerked her hand away. Maybe the baby wasn't the only thing left of their previous relationship after all—yet one more thing she didn't know how to feel about.

To give herself something to do, she reached into the bag and pulled out a fruit-and-yogurt parfait. "Thanks," she murmured as she popped off the top. "This was really thoughtful of you."

"No problem." His voice sounded strained, but she was too busy digging into her breakfast to wonder why.

As MATT PULLED UP TO a red light, he glanced at Camille out of the corner of his eye and nearly groaned. Her hair was a wild halo around her face, and the coffee and food had put a rosy tint in her pale cheeks, a tint that—combined with her hair—reminded him too much of what she looked like after a long session of lovemaking. His hands clenched the steering wheel as he felt himself harden, and he cursed the fact that she could arouse him so easily. But from the moment she'd opened the door to her motel room in her skimpy purple robe, he'd been remembering what it felt like to touch her.

To kiss her.

To make love to her.

In the few weeks they'd been together, he'd taken great delight in sliding his hands under that robe to caress her long, lean body. Seeing it again—on her— was like a slap in the face. Or a match to his libido.

Part of him had wanted nothing more than to grab her and lift her against him until her fabulous legs were wrapped around his waist and he was once again inside her. She was pregnant with his child, after all. It wasn't like they wouldn't have a future connection.

But at the same time, he didn't want to go there. Or, at least, he told himself he didn't. Camille had taken off without a backward glance once—what was to say she wouldn't do it again? Especially if he pressured her for sex.

No, this situation was difficult and chaotic enough without adding extra stress into the mix. Better to just leave things alone for a while—no need to invite more chaos because he had a difficult time controlling himself around her.

The drive to the doctor's office was made in almost complete silence—except for the soft murmurs of appreciation Camille gave every once in a while as she devoured the fruit-and-yogurt parfait he'd bought her. By the time they arrived at the tall glass-and-chrome building that housed his friend's practice, a line of sweat was running down Matt's back and he wanted nothing so much as to escape back to his simple, organized office.

Camille shot him an amused look as Matt pulled up to the circular driveway near the door. "I'm pregnant, not an invalid, you know."

"I never said you were.

"Just go park—I'm perfectly capable of walking a few hundred feet. I spent the past few weeks doing just that in Italy."

With Stefano. She didn't say the words, but they echoed in Matt's head anyway—a reminder of just how easy she'd found it to leave him—and replace him. Clenching his teeth against the thought, he murmured, "Humor me."

"Look, Matt—"

"Camille, go sit on the bench. I'll be back to get you in a minute."

"But—"

"I know you're a big girl. I know you can do this all by yourself. But the fact is, you're not by yourself anymore. I'm a part of this baby's life, too, so you might as well deal with it. Now, get *out* of the car."

His tone must have been firmer than he'd intended, because her eyes widened in a very un-Camille-like fashion. But she didn't say another word, just gathered up her purse and the trash from her breakfast and climbed from the car.

He was just thinking that perhaps he'd been a little too harsh when she slammed the door behind her so hard that his customized, lovingly restored '68 Mustang shook from the impact. He grinned as he pulled away—had he really thought Camille could be so easily cowed?

After parking the car what felt like a mile away, he hustled toward the building—unsure what he would find when he got there. The Camille he knew was more than capable of taking off without him when she was annoyed—either heading up to the doctor's office on her own or actually just taking off down the street. But when he got to the front of the building, she was sitting on the little stone bench near the front door, eyes closed and head resting against the wall behind her.

He paused for a moment, studied her. With her eyes closed and her face relaxed, she looked young and vulnerable—barely old enough to have a child, despite the fact that they'd celebrated her thirty-second birthday a few months ago, when they'd been together.

He didn't make a sound, but she must have sensed him because her eyes opened and she sat up abruptly. He watched, fascinated, as her mask descended—the carefree, smiling face he'd grown to expect from her when they'd been dating. Why hadn't he ever noticed before that she wrapped it around her like armor—just another way to keep the world outside from getting close to her? From seeing the real her.

A frisson of unease worked its way down Matt's spine as he wondered, for the first time, if there really was more to Camille than he'd ever expected.

"I didn't know the doctor's name or suite number."

And there she was, the woman who would as soon tell him to go to hell as look at him when he pissed her off, making sure he didn't read too much into the fact that she'd waited for him. "Maybe I did that on purpose," he answered.

"No doubt." She stood and headed into the building, figuring—he was sure—that he would follow. Which he did.

"His name is Rick D'Amato—he's in suite 370." He punched the button for the elevator.

"And you went to grad school with him?"

"Not with him," he said. "We were at Columbia at the same time—in different disciplines. Obviously."

"Obviously." She smirked. "You know, I just can't see you in New York."

"I like New York. There's always something to do, something to see."

"But it's so chaotic."

"There is that—but, hey, I have nothing against organized chaos."

"Just unorganized chaos."

"Exactly."

The elevator dinged and he held the door for her with a smile. She had such a quick mind that it was easy to verbally spar with her—in the months she'd been gone, he'd forgotten how much he'd liked that about her. The fact that she never pulled her punches, and didn't expect him to pull his.

"So, if you were in totally different disciplines—how did you meet Rick?"

"We played on the same intramural baseball team. He has a hell of a curve ball."

"Something every obstetrician needs."

"He's a great doctor—graduated in the top ten his year at Columbia. Friend or not, I wouldn't bring you here otherwise." It was important that she knew that, that she understood how seriously he took her health—and the baby's.

"Chill out, Matt. I was only teasing." She headed up to the counter, pulling out her identification as she went.

He hung back, though it cost him. He wanted to take care of checking her in, wanted to take care of everything for her—for his baby—but as the receptionist handed her a clipboard full of forms, it struck home how little he really knew about Camille.

Oh, he knew that she was an incredible artist. That she was fun and exciting and had a sense of humor that could cut like a scalpel. But as he sat, watching her fill out forms on her family and personal history, he realized he didn't have a clue about any aspect of her personal life. He didn't know anything about what had made Camille the crazy gypsy he'd fallen for—hook, line and sinker.

The knowledge grated. He didn't have much time to brood over it, however, because his old friend chose that moment to pop his head out of the door between the inner and outer offices. "Hey, Matt, come on back. I've been waiting for you two."

"How are you?" he asked Rick, as the doctor escorted them back to his office.

"I'm good. Busy, but good. Can't complain." He extended a hand to Camille. "It's nice to meet you, Camille. Congratulations on your pregnancy."

Camille's full lips twisted wryly. "Thanks."

"So, Matt didn't give me all the details on the phone." He gestured for them to sit, then walked around to the business side of the desk and did the same. "What was the date of your last period?"

"January 27."

He grabbed a little spinny wheel out of his desk drawer and Matt watched, fascinated, as Rick shifted it around. "You're gunning for a November baby, then. Cool. You're due on November 4." He held the wheel out so they both could see the date.

Sheer astonishment rocketed up Matt's spine as he stared at the little arrow pointing toward the beginning of November. November 4. He would be a father on November 4. God, he could barely wrap his mind around it. Sure, he'd been planning for the baby from the second the shock wore off last night, but still, knowing Camille was pregnant wasn't the same as having an actual date when the baby would be born.

November 4 his whole world would change—and he had no idea how he felt about it.

"So, does that sound good, Matt?"

Rick's voice brought him back to the present with a resounding thud. Glancing at his friend, he realized he had no idea what the man had just asked him. "I'm sorry, what?"

"I'm going to take Camille into one of the exam rooms, check her out, and then you can meet us in the ultrasound room."

"Uh, sure." Then the words sunk in. "Ultrasound, already? But she's barely three months along yet."

"It's standard procedure, Matt. We do it at every first visit, just to ensure that the pregnancy is viable."

"Viable. What does that mean?"

Rick smiled indulgently. "Nothing, man. Don't worry about it, okay? I'll talk you through it."

"Do you think something's wrong?"

"Not at all."

"But you said—"

"Matt, come on." Camille stood and starting pulling him toward the door. "It's normal. Rick's just being *organized,* making sure everything is going the way it should. Everything's fine."

He wasn't convinced. "Then why can't I be in the room when he examines you? I have questions—"

"Because, I don't really think you need to see me with my feet in stirrups and Rick between my legs with a speculum, okay?"

He froze, could feel his face draining of color even as he admired her candor. "Oh. You mean *that* kind of examination."

Rick didn't even bother to hide his laughter. "Yes, that kind." He pointed him toward the waiting room.

"I'll have a nurse come get you before we do the sonogram." Then he headed down the hall with an amused Camille.

Matt made his way awkwardly back down to the waiting room, not liking the sudden feeling of being superfluous. Sure, he had no desire to sit in on Camille's pelvic exam, but still, it felt strange to be relegated to the sidelines. He glanced around the empty room, wondered if all fathers were sent out here, or just the ones who weren't an active part of the life of their baby's mother?

Were all fathers really so unnecessary? He sank down onto one of the cushy waiting-room chairs and tried to come to grips with the fact that for the next few months, he really didn't have an important role in the whole drama that was about to unfold. He'd done his job, and now he just needed to sit back and wait for the baby to come out. Everything that went on now, went on inside Camille's body. She was the one in the driver's seat. The one in control.

For a man who had always prided himself on his ability to make order from chaos and control any situation, the realization didn't sit well. Any more than did the idea that Camille could—and probably would—get restless feet sometime in the next six months.

Because the idea of her taking off with his baby still inside of her made him feel vaguely ill, he tried to find something else to concentrate on. But the magazines were all geared toward women and he really wasn't interested in garnering the latest fashion tips.

Picking up a baby magazine, he flipped it open to an article discussing sudden infant death syndrome—and dropped it so quickly that he gave himself a paper cut.

How many things was he supposed to worry about at one time, anyway? Wasn't there enough to focus on during a pregnancy without borrowing trouble from *after* the birth?

He ended up tapping his feet nervously, counting down the seconds until he could get back to Camille. Rick had laughed at his concern that something was wrong with the baby, but he was the one who'd used the word *viable*. How was a guy supposed to relax with that hanging over his head? He'd finally wrapped his mind around the idea that Camille was pregnant, and now suddenly, Rick was telling him that it might not last?

What kind of doctor did that? What kind of friend spooked him like that, and then left him cooling his jets in the waiting room? The next time he had Rick on a baseball field, he was going to make the man—

"Mr. Jenkins?" A nurse called his name from the doorway, and he shot out of his chair like a puppet on a very short string. "You can come back now."

Thank God. If he'd had to wait much longer, he might have stroked out right in the middle of his good friend's waiting room.

CHAPTER FOUR

"DO YOU WANT TO GET SOME lunch?" Matt asked as they drove back toward her motel room.

"No, thanks. I'm not hungry." Camille's mind was going in circles, her head throbbing, and all she could think about was the image she had just seen on the sonogram screen. Tiny, so tiny that she'd had to squint to see it, but there all the same. A baby. A new life, snuggled into her uterus where it belonged, with its little heart beating up a storm. A completely viable pregnancy, Rick had announced with a wide grin. The baby looked perfect.

Her baby. Matt's baby. She didn't know what to think, how to feel. In twenty-eight weeks she was going to be a mother and she had no idea what that meant. It wasn't as if she'd had a good example growing up—or any example really. Just— She slammed the door on the memories, refusing to bring them out right then, not when it was all she could do to just sit quietly in the car as Matt went over everything Rick had told them.

"You need to eat, Camille. You heard Rick—you're healthy, but you need to gain a few pounds to help support the baby."

"I heard him. But I had breakfast less than two hours ago—how much do you expect me to eat?"

"Well, at least let me pick you up something before I drop you back at the motel." He glanced at the clock. "I have a meeting in a little over an hour, so I need to head back to work. But I've got your vitamin prescription— I'll drop it off at the pharmacy on my way to the office and pick it up at the end of the day."

"There's no rush. Rick gave me enough samples to last for two months or so."

"Still, it's better to have them on hand for when you need them. Also, I thought maybe you'd like to go to an art store tonight or tomorrow? Maybe you could look around a little, find an alternative to the oil paints that won't hurt the baby. Rick said—"

She gritted her teeth and tried not to scream, but it wasn't easy—not when Matt seemed intent on taking over every aspect of her life. If she heard *Rick said* one more time, she was going to forget that she was a pacifist and take a swing at Matt. "It's no big deal."

"Of course it is. The fumes can—"

"It's not like I'm planning on busting out the canvas today. The art supply store can wait a little while—as can lunch."

"But, Camille, you need—"

"I know what I need! I'm a grown woman who's been taking care of herself for most of her life. I have a rental car, I have a motel room. I have an ATM card and a relatively healthy checking account. When I'm hungry, I'll eat. When I'm ready to paint, I'll figure out what I want to use. And when I need more vitamins, I will go get them. So lay off, okay?"

Matt's jaw snapped shut with an audible click and for a few minutes blessed silence reigned in the car. Laying her head back against the headrest, Camille closed her eyes and tried to drift off. She was so tired—she couldn't remember ever being this tired. And Matt's constant nagging about what she needed to do and eat and think was only making her more exhausted.

She knew he was a planner, knew he liked to map things out far in advance as opposed to flying by the seat of his pants, as she was wont to do. But this was too much, even for him. He was borrowing trouble where there wasn't any, trying to fix something that wasn't broken. And it was driving her *insane*.

Still, when he pulled up in front of her motel, she couldn't help feeling a little bad for snapping at him. In his own way he was only trying to help—it wasn't his fault that all his plans were slowly freaking her out. How could he know that all she wanted was blessed silence and a chance to assimilate all the ideas currently running rampant in her head? She'd never told him.

Turning to him with a sigh, Camille laid a light hand over his, where it rested on the steering wheel. "Look, Matt, I didn't mean to bite your head off. I just—"

"It's okay."

"You were just trying to help and I totally blew up. I'm sorry."

When he finally turned his head, it was with a contrite grin. "Nothing to be sorry about. I keep talking about this pregnancy, but forget the most basic stuff. Like how tired you're supposed to be in the first trimester—even without the jet-lag. Go get some sleep and I'll call to check on you in a few hours."

She searched his face for a minute, but found no sign of upset—just a rueful resignation that all was not going to go according to his master plan. Of course, now that she'd gotten her way, she couldn't help thinking that it was kind of sweet, how much interest Matt was taking in her and her pregnancy. A lot of guys would have been horrified to have an ex-girlfriend drop in, pregnant and unannounced. Matt had simply absorbed the news and then started making decisions that he thought would keep the baby healthy and safe.

He was a stand-up guy, and though she hadn't planned this pregnancy, she could have done a lot worse for the father of her baby. Impulsively, she leaned over and kissed his cheek.

Matt froze for a second, then turned so that his lips brushed against hers. Once, twice, so softly that it felt like a feather whispering over her mouth. And yet his touch reawakened something inside of her, a need for him that she'd sublimated but that had never really gone away.

Reaching up, she wrapped her arms around his neck and pulled him closer, until his mouth fit fully over hers. Then she sucked his lower lip between her teeth and nibbled on it, in the way she knew he loved.

He groaned, yanked her across his gearshift, and pressed her against him so that her breasts were flush with his chest, her legs straddling his as the steering wheel bit into her back.

But she didn't care, the pain barely registering as his lips raced across her cheek and down her neck to the pulse point at the hollow of her throat. She moaned, let her head fall back while he licked at her favorite erogenous zone. Heat raced up her spine, her fingers tangling in Matt's hair as she started moving anxiously above him. Against him.

He felt so good, made her feel so good, that she couldn't help wanting to forget the nearly three months that stretched between them. Couldn't help wanting to take this attraction as far as she could and to say to hell with the consequences. They'd been good together once, they would be again. And if it complicated things, they would deal—they were grown-ups after all.

Twisting her fingers in his hair, she yanked Matt's mouth back up to hers and devoured him. He tasted just as she remembered—like lemon and mint and the deepest, darkest chocolate. Familiar, comforting and yet so exciting she could swear she heard her brain begin to sizzle. Dipping into his mouth, she stroked his tongue with her own and—

Matt wrenched his mouth away with another groan. She whimpered, tried to drag him back, but he lifted her and set her back on the passenger seat.

"We can't do this here," he muttered, his voice dark and growly and so sexy that it took all her willpower not to climb back into his lap. He was breathing heavily—maybe even more heavily than she was. His dark auburn hair was tousled from her fingers and his dark eyes were burning with the same need licking its way through her. "People are everywhere."

For the first time since Matt's lips had met her own, Camille became truly aware of where they were—in Matt's car, parked in front of the door to her motel room, and people were, indeed, everywhere.

"Do you—" She cleared her throat. "Do you want to come up to my room?"

He shook his head regretfully. "I've got a meeting in a little more than half an hour."

"Right. Your meeting. I forgot." She felt her cheeks blaze and for a moment wanted nothing more than for the ground to open and swallow her. She'd been the one to break up with Matt, yet now she was practically begging him to take her back. It was embarrassing, especially considering the fact that he'd been able to pull away when she was so far gone she would have let him take her in the front seat of his car. Not to mention the fact that he'd turned down an invitation into her bed because he had a *meeting*.

Maybe it was childish to expect him to drop everything to be with her, but she didn't understand how he could run so hot and cold. How he could be so controlled after he'd all but ripped her clothes off in the front of his car?

For a minute, she couldn't help thinking of the cool blonde she'd run into at his house the night before, couldn't help wondering how serious she and Matt were.

"Right, of course, I'm sorry." She fumbled for the door handle. "I'm tired anyway." She scrambled out of the car. "I guess I'll see you…whenever."

"I'll call you later, Camille."

"Sure. Later." She started to slam the door, but stopped as Matt held out a hand to her.

"Make sure you get some lunch—and pick out a place for dinner. I'll take you out."

"You don't have to do that, Matt."

His eyes grew even darker, hotter, as he growled, "I want to. Now stop arguing and go get some rest. I'll talk to you later." He leaned across the seat, grabbed her hand. Squeezed. And suddenly she didn't feel nearly so uncertain.

Stepping back, she slammed the car door and watched as he drove away. He waved right before he turned the corner and her hand lifted automatically in response, though he had already turned and couldn't see her.

Then, refusing to think about what that kiss had or hadn't done to their relationship, she headed up the stairs to her motel room, where she flopped onto the bed and promptly fell asleep, fully dressed.

FOR THE FIRST TIME THAT he could remember, Matt had a difficult time keeping his mind on his job. During the meeting with the new clients, he screwed up no less than four times—on minor stuff that any architectural grad student should have a strong grasp of.

Right around the fourth mess-up, he caught his best friend and partner, Reece Sandler, staring at him as if he'd lost his mind. And when, a few minutes later—after he'd screwed up again—Reece mouthed, "What the hell is wrong with you?" he didn't even take offense.

How could he? He was so far off his game that it was a miracle the clients hadn't given up and walked out. He wouldn't blame them if they did—despite the copious amount of work he and Reece had put into designing the new Japanese skyscraper. The building was tall and monolithic, with incredible angles that let in an abundance of light and a roof that was different from anything else in the business. He and his partner considered it one of their best designs. What had started out as a brainstorming session a couple of years ago had turned into what they hoped would soon be the Makati Tower.

Which was why, when the meeting was over and the Makati Corporation representatives were on their way out, Matt didn't object to letting Reece show them to the elevator on his own. From the time they had set out their shingle eleven years before, Reece had always been the deal-closer. Funny, polished and extroverted, he rarely failed to bring the client around to their way of thinking. He was a hell of an architect, too, but he was definitely the salesman in their partnership.

Matt was the detail guy, the one who took Reece's sometimes fantastical ideas and made them work. He was the problem-solver, the number cruncher, the one who made the difficult easy and the impossible possible. Which was why it sucked that he'd been off his game today—when Hiro Makati himself had asked about the methods that went into creating the sharp angles that were the building's cornerstones, it should have been a slam dunk for him to answer. After all, he'd designed them.

Instead, all he'd been able to think about was Camille and how she'd looked when he'd driven away from her after the doctor's appointment.

Beautiful, stunned and a little insecure—which was not a word he normally associated with his former lover—she'd touched his heart. Again. After he'd promised himself that he wouldn't let it happen, wouldn't let her get inside him this time so that she could just walk away again. And he'd blown it, already.

She'd been back from Italy less than twenty-four hours and he was already hungering to take her to bed, to let her back into his life. To try again, even though he was sure it wouldn't work out. They were too different— he liked security, craved it, and she was the woman her high school graduating class voted most likely to sail around the world. Even more, she was the woman who *had* sailed around the world—more than once, while he'd always been the guy to keep his feet planted firmly on the ground.

How the two of them were ever going to raise a child together, he didn't know. But he was smart enough to know that complicating that job with a renewal of their sexual relationship was definitely not a good idea. Eventually things would burn out between them and then where would they be—bitter and angry with each other at worst, awkward and uncomfortable at best.

No, it was better to keep things simple between them. To keep things platonic. Besides, he couldn't afford to mess with Camille—she was bad for his peace of mind, bad for his organization. Chaos followed her around and, even worse, worked its way into his own life when he was with her. His disastrous performance at the meeting today was proof of that.

Because he felt guilty as hell—he and Reece had worked too hard on this design to watch it go up in smoke because he couldn't get his ducks in a row—Matt didn't even try to dodge Reece's incredulous look when he came back into the conference room.

"You want to tell me what that was all about?" Reece demanded, leaning against the table. "And don't tell me 'nothing,' because I've known you since we were freshmen at UT and I have *never* seen you screw up like that. Not once in damn near eighteen years of friendship."

For a split second, Matt didn't know what he wanted to say. After all, he'd yet to come to grips with everything that had changed in his life in the past twenty-four hours and the idea of talking about it… Still, this was Reece and he knew his friend well enough to know that he didn't let go once he'd sunk his teeth into something—in this case, Matt's uncharacteristic screw-ups.

Not sure what he was going to say, he opened up his mouth and the words "Camille's pregnant" flew out before he could stop them.

Reece didn't immediately respond, just sat there and blinked at him for a few long seconds. "Camille? The woman you were dating a few months back?"

"Yes."

"The one you moped around about for weeks?"

"Yes."

"She's pregnant?"

"Yes." He was beginning to feel like a parrot.

"With your kid?"

"Well, yeah. I don't think I'd be this stressed out if it was someone else's."

"Hey, when did this happen?"

Matt stared at his friend incredulously. "Excuse me?"

"Not the pregnant thing, the you-finding-out thing."

"Oh. Yesterday."

"So this is what you needed the gynecologist's number for?"

"Well, it sure as hell wasn't for me."

"Yeah, but I figured one of your sisters was looking for a new doctor or something. It never occurred to me that you'd gotten a woman pregnant, but at least everything is making a bit more sense now."

"I'm glad it makes sense to you, because my head is so screwed up that I can barely see straight."

Reece reached over, clamped a hand on his shoulder. "Tell me."

He didn't have a clue where to start, so for the first time in his life he opened his mouth and just rambled. "I fell for her the first time I saw her. She was doing sidewalk art a few blocks from the UT stadium, keeping the fans amused as we killed time before the game."

"I remember. You were twenty minutes late for kick-off and when you finally showed up you looked like you'd been hit in the head with a two-by-four."

"That's how I felt. I hung out with her for over an hour, even paid her twenty bucks to do a caricature of me." She'd drawn him in a suit and tie, a huge briefcase clutched in one hand and an even bigger pocket watch in the other. He'd been amazed at the astuteness of her drawing, especially since he'd been dressed in faded jeans and an old UT shirt. "Then I stood around, trying to get her number as she drew a bunch of pictures for other people.

"She finally gave me her cell number and I couldn't wait to call her. I told myself it was no big deal, that I was just having fun with a beautiful woman, but I was sinking fast and was too dumb to know it."

"There's nothing wrong with having feelings for a smart, talented, beautiful woman, Matt."

He laughed, but there was no humor in the sound. "There is when you know going in that she isn't going to stick around. That she's a gypsy who goes wherever the spirit takes her."

He stood up, not sure where he was going but knowing that he couldn't sit still for one more second—not if he had to keep talking about Camille. "Anyway, I broke the rules."

"You had rules for your relationship?" Reece's voice was incredulous. "That's a bit much, even for you, isn't it?"

"She had rules. I went along with them because—" He walked over to the window that looked out over the city he'd been born and raised in. Down below, cars raced through the narrow downtown streets as pedestrians darted in and out of traffic. "Because I was willing to do whatever it took to be with her. Even let her go. Except—"

"Except what?" Reece prompted from across the room.

"Except let her go. When it was time for her next great adventure, I asked her to stay. Hell, I nearly begged her. It's humiliating, in retrospect, to think about how I pleaded for more time with her. Even after she left, I couldn't believe she was gone. Couldn't believe that she didn't feel the same way about me that I felt about her. I called her for weeks, left messages on her cell. She never called me back."

He glanced behind him at Reece. "Pathetic, right?"

His friend looked uncomfortable. "No, not pathetic, exactly. Just—"

"Stupid? Obsessive? Stalkerish? Ridiculous? Pick the adjective of your choice."

"Desperate, maybe?"

Matt groaned. "Thanks. I always knew I could count on you to kick me while I was down."

"Hey, you asked."

"Yeah, well, it was rhetorical."

"It didn't sound rhetorical." Reece paused, then asked, "So how'd Camille tell you?"

"She showed up in the middle of my date with Ariane and announced that she was three months pregnant."

"Ouch. Your woman doesn't believe in beating around the bush, does she?"

"No. Not at all. And she's not my woman."

"You're gaga over her and she's carrying your kid— I'm not sure how much more your woman she could be."

"It's not like that. That part of our relationship is over." Even as he said it, he could feel Camille's long, lithe body pressed against him. Could smell her wild strawberry scent, though it had been hours since he'd seen her.

"Why not? She cared enough to come back and tell you she was pregnant. That has to count for something."

"I don't think so. She doesn't want any help from me, doesn't want anything from me. She just thought I had a right 'to know about the baby.'" He used his fingers to make quotes in the air.

"Yeah, but what do you want?"

"I want to wake up tomorrow and find out this was all a bad dream."

A long, uneasy silence stretched between them before Reece finally said, "Well, if that's really what you want, I'd say you're on the right path. You say she doesn't want anything from you, right?"

Matt's hands clenched into fists at the reminder. "Right."

"So let her go. Problem solved."

He whirled around in outrage. "Did you not hear me? She's pregnant with my baby. It's not like I can just walk away from that."

"Men do it all the time." There was an echo of pain in Reece's voice, a reminder of how he'd walked away from his wife, Sarah, when she'd been pregnant with their daughter, Rose. Sure, he'd been grieving and wasn't seeing his life clearly, but it had nearly killed Reece, and Matt had no intention of making the same mistake.

"Yeah, well, I don't. She needs me. My *kid* needs me."

"But what do *you* need?"

Matt turned back to the window, to the hundreds of people down below who seemed to know exactly where they were going. Two days ago, he'd been one of them, but now he was adrift. Lost. More confused than he could ever remember being.

"I don't know, Reece. I just don't know."

He knew he wanted to be there for Camille, and for their child. But at the same time, he wasn't ready to risk his heart again—at least not on the woman who had so recently stomped all over it with a wink and a smile.

"You don't have to have an answer for everything today."

Reece's quiet observation broke into Matt's thoughts, brought him back to the present with a thud. "Of course I know that."

"Do you?"

At the question, he concentrated extra hard on watching the pedestrians down below in their suits and jeans, their bohemian skirts and beads.

Part of him wanted to be down there, amid the anonymous throngs of humanity. Connected, but not. Part of a whole, but separate, as well. Up here, with Reece's too-sharp eyes and even more pointed questions, there was nowhere for him to hide.

"Don't be stupid. Having a baby isn't like deciding what's for lunch. There are a million details to be taken care of, a million decisions that have to be made. A lot of those decisions I'm not even equipped to make yet. I haven't done the research, haven't looked at both sides—"

"That's not what I meant and you know it." Reece crossed the room to the little minifridge in the corner, whipped out two cans of soda. He tossed one to Matt, before popping the top on the second and taking a long drink.

Matt followed suit.

"Look, Matt, you've always been the guy with the answers. The one who knows what to do when nobody else does. Maybe it's because you were the only guy in the house and you felt you always had to have the answers for your mom and your sisters. Maybe it's because you're the most conscientious, detail-oriented guy I know. Who knows? But the fact is, you *always* know what to do."

"Not this time."

Reece laughed. "Of course not this time! This isn't like designing a building or running an office or impressing clients—any more than it's about fixing your mom's sink *or* her finances. This is about you, about *your* life. Even more important, it's about the life of your child. Of course you don't know what to do yet.

"You know, it may sound corny, but there's a reason you get nine months before a baby comes. It takes that long to figure things out. Hell, sometimes it takes even longer."

"I don't know what to do about Camille." He blurted out the truth of what was really bothering him. "I mean,

I'm worried about what will happen when the baby comes, but more than that, I just can't figure out what my relationship with Camille is supposed to be like now."

"What do you want it to be like?" Reece asked, after taking a long sip of his drink.

"I don't know! Part of me wants nothing more than to get her into the nearest bed and keep her there for as long as she'll let me, but another part figures that's the worst move I could possibly make."

"I'm not sure if I understand your reasoning there. She's the mother of your child—shouldn't you be attracted to her?"

"No! I mean, not now. Not again." Matt shook his head emphatically. "Things won't work between us, long-term—we've already figured that much out. So what good will it do if we start back on the same path we were on before? All that's going to do is cause hurt feelings and make it that much more difficult to be objective about the baby."

"It's your child. You're not supposed to be objective."

"You know what I mean. Visitation, child support— those types of things. I need a clear head when we talk about all that and I won't have it if I'm sleeping with Camille—or pissed off that I'm not sleeping with her anymore."

"All right, then. It sounds like you've made up your mind. Keep things as platonic between you as possible."

Matt stared at Reece for long seconds, then nodded. "You're right. That's definitely my plan. I don't need the extra chaos she adds to my life—you saw what happened with the meeting today. I'll just be the supportive friend and father of the baby—"

"Don't you mean 'baby daddy'?" Reece asked with a smirk.

Matt crumpled up his empty soda can and lobbed it across the room at his friend. "Very funny."

Reece ducked, laughing. "Just saying."

"Yeah, I know what you're saying."

"But do you know what *you're* saying?"

"What does that mean?"

"It means Camille's a fabulous woman and if I were in your shoes..." He shook his head. "If I were in your shoes, I might sit back and enjoy the ride. Let the future take care of itself."

"Because that worked so well for you, right?" As soon as the words had left his mouth, Matt regretted them. Reece had suffered a lot in the past couple of years— between losing his first wife in a car accident, nearly giving up Rose, almost losing Sarah and their unborn child. There was no need to rub it in.

"Actually, it did work out pretty well for me, thank you very much. It might do you well to remember that." And with that cryptic comment, Reece gathered up his papers and headed for the door, leaving Matt staring after him, his confidence regarding his decision suddenly on very shaky ground.

CHAPTER FIVE

CAMILLE WOKE UP IN A MUCH better mood than she went to sleep in. With the dregs of jet-lag finally dissipating and dinner with a handsome man who just happened to be the father of her child on the horizon, it was turning out to be a pretty good day.

After a long, luxurious shower and hair wash, she sat on the bed in her towel—television blaring—and painted her toes a frosty blue. As she stroked the brush over one toenail and then another, she couldn't help wondering how much longer she'd be able to do this for herself. How much longer until advancing stages of pregnancy made it difficult, if not impossible, to bend at the waist.

Surprisingly, the idea wasn't as abhorrent to her as it had been just a couple of days before. Maybe it was because she was finally getting used to the idea, which had seemed like a far-fetched nightmare when she'd taken three pregnancy tests, just to be sure.

Or maybe it was because she'd seen the baby on the ultrasound, had heard its little heartbeat echo throughout the room. In her whole life, she'd never felt anything more powerful than that one moment, when she saw— with crystal clarity—what she and Matt had made.

The image had influenced him, as well. As Rick was explaining what they were seeing, she had stolen a quick glimpse at Matt, had realized he looked as bowled over as she felt. It was an odd realization about the man who had fathered her child—and who always seemed to be in such complete control, of himself and the world around him.

Closing the nail polish, Camille flopped back on the bed, wet hair and all, and waited for the polish to dry. As she stared at the ceiling, she ran her hands over her stomach, tried to determine if it had grown rounder in the twelve weeks since she'd gotten pregnant. It didn't feel any different, but maybe she was just deluding herself. How long before she started to show? How long before her life changed forever?

Twenty-eight weeks, if she wanted to be exact. The baby would be born in approximately twenty-eight weeks and then there would be no going back. She would be responsible for another human being, a tiny life that was dependent almost exclusively on her for its survival.

The thought made her sick to her stomach, but at the same time a totally contradictory excitement was building in her. Yes, she might mess up. Hell, she probably would mess up, but there was a chance—if she was careful—that she could do this thing right. That she could give her baby everything she had lacked as a child. That, with Matt's help, she could build a real family for this baby.

Matt. She thought back to the kiss in the car and felt herself flush a little, though not with embarrassment. How could he still manage to turn her on so completely, when it had been three months since they'd gone their separate ways? And how could she deal with him as the father of her child, when all she really wanted to do was jump his very delectable bones?

But who could blame her? Matt was a fabulous lover—sexy, inventive, incredibly generous and enthusiastic. He'd surprised her more than once in bed, in the best possible ways.

Her breasts, already sensitive from the pregnancy, grew heavy at the memories and Camille forced her mind to other things. It wasn't easy, but it was necessary—unless she wanted to be one giant ball of lust by the time Matt showed up.

Not that that would necessarily be a bad thing, she mused, as she pushed off the bed. At least not judging by the hair-straightening, toe-curling kiss they'd engaged in earlier that day. She'd been kissed by a lot of men in her travels and never had she found one who took her over so completely. Who crawled inside of her and gave her everything she was craving, including things she had no idea she wanted.

On the television, the program changed to the local six o'clock news and she sprang into action at the same time the news anchors did. Matt would be here in thirty minutes and she was about as far from ready as she could get—unless, of course, he was planning on staying in.

After running some product through her hair—with her curls, that was the best she could do—she slipped into a short-sleeved purple dress that hugged her from breast to knee. It was one of her favorites and she figured this was her last chance to wear it for a while—pretty soon, her stomach would make the dress's silhouette completely unattractive.

When she was dressed, she did a quick once-over in the mirror, to make sure everything was in the proper place. It was, but when she got to her face, she stopped, transfixed, by the strange softness in her eyes.

Reaching a hand out, she touched the reflection of her face in the mirror. Traced a finger over the softened curve of her lower lip, the relaxed slope of her normally tense jaw. Who was this woman who seemed so open and unguarded? This woman who was contemplating settling down, even for a little while?

She looked happy and nervous and a little overwhelmed all at the same time. Camille took a step back, wondered what was happening to her. Was she really going to lower her defenses? Was she really—

A knock at the door interrupted her reverie. Shaking her head, Camille attempted to drop the deep philosophy—at least for now. After all, things were going to work out how they were going to work out and there really wasn't all that much she could do to control them. Not now, when the ball had already been set into motion.

Throwing the door open, she found Matt on the other side—tall, handsome, smiling the half smile that always made her shiver. Without giving herself time to think, she threw her arms around him and brushed a kiss over his lips.

His hands came to her waist and she thought, for a minute, that he was going to pull her closer. Instead, he pushed her away—just a little bit, but enough to get the message across.

Pulling back, she looked at him uncertainly. "What's wrong, Matt? Bad day?" She smoothed a hand over the line that had formed between his eyes.

"No. It was a great day, actually. We made a big presentation to a new client that went very well."

"That's great! Congratulations."

"Thanks." He glanced behind her, into her motel room. "Are you ready to go?"

"Sure. Absolutely. Just let me get my purse."

When she turned back toward the bed, where she'd dropped her purse for easy access, Camille felt as if her smile was painted on. Maybe she was making too big a deal of things, but Matt seemed distant. Unapproachable. Very different from the man she was used to.

As they walked to the car, she asked again, "Are you sure everything's okay?"

He looked at her in apparent surprise. "Of course. Why?"

She started to shrug it off, to put the blame on herself for being too sensitive. But that was exactly what her mother would have done, taken the blame when she'd done absolutely nothing wrong.

The thought nearly froze her in her tracks, had her blurting out her thoughts without censoring them. "You seem distant, like you don't really want to be here."

"Of course I want to be here. Where else would I be?"

His answer, meant to reassure her, did the exact opposite—partly because the smile he'd given her hadn't reached his eyes and partly because it stank of him patronizing her.

Back stiff at the thought, she scanned the motel parking lot for his Mustang, but didn't see the cherry-red convertible anywhere. "I brought my other car," he said, leading her to an ice-blue BMW Roadster parked near the stairs.

"When did you get this?" she asked.

"About six weeks ago. Of course, if I'd known I was going to be a father in a few months, I would have picked something with a backseat."

His words hit like barbs, though she wasn't sure whether they were meant to or not. They were just one more reminder of how much she was disrupting his calm, organized life.

"It's really nice," she murmured inanely, as he held the door open for her.

"Thanks."

They rode to the restaurant in an uncomfortable silence that was as different from their regular sparring as it could get. More than once Camille tried to initiate conversation, but she was shot down every time. By the time they pulled into the parking lot of her favorite Mexican restaurant, her nerves were frayed and her temper was starting to sizzle.

Still, she knew how to behave in public, she reminded herself as they were shown to a table, all her joy in the evening with Matt slowly leaking away. Obviously something had upset him and if he didn't want to talk about it, then he didn't have to. She'd leave him to brood and focus on enjoying her meal instead.

She perused the menu slowly, did her best to calm herself down as she decided between spinach enchiladas and a chicken chile relleno. But by the time the waitress had brought their drinks and taken their order, she couldn't take it anymore.

"What is wrong with you?" she demanded, just as he shoved a chip loaded with salsa into his mouth.

He chewed slowly, methodically, then leveled his dark, brooding stare across the table at her. "Nothing. Why?" He shoveled in another chip.

"You're acting like you're getting a root canal—or worse, like you'd prefer to be getting one."

He choked on the chip, and had to reach, eyes watering, for his drink to wash it down. She watched him suffer without the least bit of sympathy—glad that, for now at least, the regular, kick-ass Camille seemed to be in charge, instead of that vulnerable, doe-eyed woman in the mirror.

Just remembering that woman—and the excitement she'd felt getting ready for this date—had Camille's blood ready to boil.

"You're being absurd, Camille."

"Don't do that. Don't treat me like I'm some stupid little child who has no idea what she's talking about. You're different tonight. Harsher."

Matt sighed, then rubbed the bridge of his nose as if she was giving him a headache. It was just one more dismissive gesture and Camille had had enough. Shoving back from the table, she picked up her purse and walked away from him.

"Hey!" He jumped up and followed her. "Where are you going?"

"To the ladies' room. Care to join me?" Her tone implied he was anything but welcome.

"Oh, sorry. I, ah—I'll wait for you at the table."

"Good idea." Her smile was sweet enough to strip the enamel off his teeth.

Camille took her time in the restroom, washed her hands a few times, tinkered with her hair and her lipstick and her earrings. She didn't know what bug had crawled up Matt's butt, but she had had just about enough of being treated like she was a pariah. Who did he think he was, kissing her like he had that morning—as if the whole world revolved around her—and then all but blowing her off tonight?

He could have canceled—it wasn't like she would have held it against him. A night alone in her motel room with a pizza and a good book would have been much preferable to this debacle. Call her crazy, but she wasn't overly impressed at being treated as if she had a particularly virulent strain of the plague.

She applied another coat of lip gloss, fluffed her hair yet again in an effort to waste more time. Truth be told, she hated playing these games, but there was no way she was giving Matt the upper hand. Once a woman did that, she could forget about ever getting it back, and she refused to be at the mercy of some man's whims. She'd had to live that way once, and would be damned if she'd voluntarily put herself into that kind of situation.

When she figured she had her temper under control again—not to mention having wasted enough time to have Matt cooling his heels—she sauntered back through the dining room to where he was waiting. Their dinners had arrived while she'd been gone, but he hadn't touched his.

Too bad his gentlemanly manners couldn't rub off on his attitude.

"Are you all right?" he asked as soon as she sat down.

"I'm fine. Why?"

"You were gone a long time. I was getting worried."

"As you can see, I'm fine. Nothing to worry about." She turned her attention to the spinach enchiladas in front of her and dug in with gusto, refusing to let him see how much his irritation had affected her appetite.

After that scintillating exchange, they ate in silence. She could feel Matt's eyes on her throughout the meal, but she refused to make eye contact. He'd started the whole Mexican standoff and she would *not* be the one who blinked first. If that made her childish, it was a label she was willing to live with—at least in this instance.

The waiter was clearing their plates before Matt broke. "Would you like dessert?" he asked quietly.

"No, thank you. I'm full." She picked up her water glass, took a long sip.

"Come on, Camille. Don't you think this is ridiculous?"

"What?" she asked him with wide-eyed innocence.

"You haven't said a word to me since you got back from the restroom."

"I was under the impression that you didn't want to talk." She raised an inquiring brow. "But if that isn't the case, then by all means, let's chat."

He ran a frustrated hand over his face. "I should have known you'd be like this."

"Me? You're the one who showed up with a chip on his shoulder the size of Mount Rushmore. Why is that, anyway?"

"I do not have a chip on my shoulder."

"Really? What would you call it, then?"

"Concern! I'm concerned, that's all."

"About what?"

"About everything. About the baby. About you. About—" He paused, took an awkward sip of his beer. "About our relationship and where it's going."

She dropped the frigid routine in a heartbeat, reached across the table and squeezed his hand. "And where do you think that is?"

"I don't know." As he looked at her, his eyes were miserable, but clear.

"Yes, you do. You just don't want to say it out loud."

Silence stretched between them and just when she was sure Matt wasn't going to answer her, he blurted out, "I don't think it should go anywhere."

They were the words she'd been expecting, ever since she'd seen his face when she opened the door of her motel room. But that didn't make them any easier to hear. "You don't want to be a part of the baby's life?"

"What? Of course I do. I wasn't talking about that."

"What were you talking about, then?"

"About us. About what's going to happen between you and me."

Of course. She sat back in her chair, regarded him with what she hoped were blank eyes. The kiss that had so invigorated her earlier that day, the one that had gotten her thinking about being with Matt, had had the opposite effect on him. He was spooked and running scared, not the least bit interested in being with her.

Because of the delicate Ariane? she wondered, then decided it didn't matter. If it wasn't Ariane now it would be some other woman later. Some woman who was nicer than Camille, more settled, more organized. More biddable.

"Is that what this is about?" she finally asked. "You think I'm ready to drag you to the altar or something? Believe me, I'm not."

"This is you we're talking about, Camille. Believe me, the altar never even crossed my mind."

Well, she'd asked for that, hadn't she? Besides, he wasn't saying anything she hadn't thought herself a million times before. Wasn't saying anything she hadn't told him multiple times, as well. She wasn't the marrying sort—she'd always known that. Why, then, was Matt's rejection hitting her so hard?

Maybe because she had begun to build her very fragile hopes around him—not for marriage, but for a relationship that lasted longer than a couple of weeks? He was the father of her child, after all. Was it so abnormal to want to be close to him?

Obviously, it was.

She cleared her throat, struggling with emotions that were threatening to overwhelm her. She took her time, beat them back. *Never let them see you cry* was more than a cliché—it was a motto she lived by.

When she finally thought she could speak without her voice trembling, she asked, "I should have known that kiss today would freak you out, make you think there was more between us than there is."

His eyes narrowed. "You mean, you weren't thinking the same thing?"

"Of course not," she lied. "Going back to a romantic relationship is just asking for complications, isn't it?"

"Exactly." He looked relieved by her logic. "With the baby coming along I think it would be better to keep things strictly platonic between us. For everybody's sake."

She nearly laughed out loud, despite the fact that his rejection hurt. *Strictly platonic?* Who was he kidding? The two of them in a room together were like gasoline and an open flame—they always had been and she sincerely doubted that impending parenthood was going to change that.

But just because they responded to each other physically didn't mean he actually wanted her—in fact, Matt had made it abundantly clear tonight that she was the last thing he wanted. Artistic, emotional, disorganized, she was probably his worst nightmare, relationship-wise. Sometime between their conversation three months ago and tonight, he must have copped to that fact.

It wasn't as if she could blame him. His point was logical, well thought-out. And correct—trying to build a relationship between them was just asking for problems later, when it all fell apart.

The misty-eyed woman she'd confronted in the mirror earlier rose up in front of her again, but Camille banished her once and for all.

"I think that's a good idea, Matt." Camille held up her water glass, toasted him. "Here's to a long, platonic friendship." She took a big sip.

"So, do you want to shake on it?" she asked, offering her palm.

Matt laughed, then enveloped her hand in his large, calloused one. "To friendship," he echoed.

"Absolutely." She pulled her hand away, pushed back from the table. "So are you ready to go? I could really use some chocolate."

"Then by all means, let's find a bakery." He dropped some money on the table and she thought briefly about insisting on paying for her share of the meal, but figured it would make her sound less than happy with their current relationship.

The rest of the evening passed in a friendly sort of companionship, with Matt buying her the biggest brownie he could find from a local shop. By the time he'd dropped her off at her motel, chocolate drunk and giggling, she'd almost convinced herself that her earlier folly had been nothing more than a dream.

It wasn't until she was lying in bed later that night, staring at the ceiling as sleep avoided her, that she had to face the truth. She was disappointed that things were on permanent hold between her and Matt. She had wanted to explore whatever it was that was between them.

But that was over and it was for the best, anyway. In the long run, things wouldn't have worked out and then the baby would be caught in the middle. No, it was better this way, definitely.

Why was she so bereft at the thought of not being with Matt, anyway? It wasn't as if she needed him or anything. She could handle whatever life threw at her— she'd been doing it for more years than she could count. Having a baby wouldn't be any different.

So, from here on out, Matt was the father of her baby, nothing more. And she'd do well to remember that. Expecting this to be a new beginning for them had obviously been a mistake, and one she wouldn't be making again.

CHAPTER SIX

SHE COULDN'T BREATHE. Camille pressed a hand to her suddenly aching chest and struggled to suck enough air into her lungs to keep her head from spinning. But no matter how hard she tried, she just couldn't seem to breathe. The dizziness got worse, until suddenly the bright, sunny apartment she was standing in looked dark and shady. Almost sinister.

"So, do you like it?" asked the property manager in her chirpy voice. It matched her bright yellow suit and shiny blond hair and did absolutely nothing to put Camille at ease.

In fact, it—along with the woman's too-perky attitude—only made Camille more uncomfortable. "I need to go outside," she gasped, the fist in her chest getting tighter with each second she spent in the apartment from hell.

She made her way shakily toward the door.

Belatedly, the woman noticed that the apartment's "cozy charm" was not working its magic on her prospective client. "Are you okay?" she asked, following Camille out of the apartment like a stray dog. "Are you feeling all right?"

"I'm fine. I just need some air."

"Are you sure? Because you look a little pale. Do you want to sit—"

"I'm fine!" Camille barked out the words, then felt bad for being so abrupt. It wasn't the woman's fault she was having a panic attack at the idea of renting an apartment. After all, she'd been perfectly fine until she'd heard the words *twelve-month lease*.

That's when her head had started to spin. *Twelve months?* She'd never stayed anywhere twelve months—at least not since she'd graduated high school and set out on her own. Hell, she'd never stayed anywhere even half that long. In college, she'd managed to stick around the same art school for a semester, finishing up classes, before her itchy feet took over. But since she'd gotten her degree—from the seventh college she'd attended—she'd never stayed in one place longer than five or six weeks. The two months she'd spent with Matt in Austin had been the longest she'd stayed anywhere—and look how that had turned out.

And now this woman wanted her to sign a twelve-month lease? That so wasn't going to happen—at least not if she wanted to avoid passing out in a trembling, nonsensical heap at the woman's feet.

Struggling to be polite, she held out a hand to the apartment manager. "Thanks so much for your time. I have a couple more properties to see and then I'll get back in touch."

"You know, we're running a special—today only. If you sign a lease before six tonight, we'll throw in a free month's rent. I'm sure, with a baby on the way—"

"Thank you. I'll keep that in mind."

Camille turned away before the woman could say anything else and made her way unsteadily to her bright red rental car, where she collapsed into the driver's seat.

Twelve months? How could she possibly consider staying here—in Austin, Texas—for twelve months? Sure, she'd psyched herself up to stay around until the baby was born. Had figured she'd take a few small trips before then, to make up for the semipermanent home base.

But twelve months? That was a year! The baby would be nearly six months by then and she'd figured they'd be long gone. She'd planned on going to the Dominican Republic this coming winter, then on to Jamaica—but neither was a place for a little baby; bad water, not enough food, less than stellar medical care.

Her breath started coming in short pants. Laying her head on the steering wheel, Camille struggled to get control of herself. But it was hard—especially when she thought about what life would be like after the baby came. She wouldn't be able to just pick up at a moment's notice, would she? Babies required attention and regular checkups with their pediatricians and stability and routine—just like Matt had tried telling her. They needed familiar things around them and—

Forget it. She gave up on the battle to stay strong and just let the panic come. It rolled over her in waves, sent shivers down her spine and made it even more difficult to catch her breath.

Maybe she was stupid to think it was a good idea to keep the baby. Maybe she should just have an abortion and get it over with—no! She couldn't do that. Not now, when she'd seen it on the ultrasound. Not now, when she and Matt had heard its little heart beat....

Matt. She hadn't seen him since he'd taken her out to dinner four nights before—and dropped the bombshell about keeping their friendship strictly platonic. He called every day to check up on her, to see how she was feeling and if she needed anything, but he hadn't stopped by again. Hadn't badgered her to eat, hadn't brought her decaf coffee or offered to take her to the art store for supplies.

At first, she hadn't noticed his absence—after all, she was used to being on her own and she hadn't come across a situation where she needed his input. But now, after four days, the fact that he hadn't come around had taken on shades of deliberation, no matter how busy he claimed to be with a new project.

Was this what she could expect from him, then? Spurts of intense attention followed by long, dry periods with a quick phone call their only contact? Was that what her baby could count on? The same thing she'd always gotten from her father? Was her baby going to end up like her?

Worse, was she somehow going to end up like her mother?

No! Of course not—she would never allow that to happen, never allow herself to sink so low that she would be any man's doormat.

Would never live in fear, waiting for her husband to come home, wondering if he *would* come home and what woman's perfume he'd be wearing when he did.

Would never put her own dreams and desires on hold because some man convinced her that taking care of him was more important than living her life.

Besides, it was crazy to get this worked up when she was still months and months away from delivering. There was no use in borrowing trouble, and certainly no use in dredging up a past that was long over.

She was being ridiculous, indulging in a snit—over Matt and having to get an apartment and the fact that her whole life was changing so quickly she could barely keep up. Besides, she and Matt hadn't discussed anything yet. Not her expectations of him, or his of her. Not his role in the baby's life. Nothing but the boundaries of their own relationship. It was ridiculous to be upset just because he wasn't hovering over her every second of the day.

It wasn't like that was what she wanted.

Determined to be a grown-up, she turned the car on and slowly backed out of her parking spot. It would be better to go see Matt, to talk with him, than to sit here attributing all kinds of nefarious, or at least murky, intentions to him.

But by the time Camille had made the fifteen-minute drive to his house, she'd all but lost her nerve. What was she going to say to him, anyway? *You've been ignoring me and I don't like it?* Geez, could she be a little more high maintenance?

Besides, what if the beautiful Ariane was in there again? How could she possibly explain her presence at his door a second time?

Stupid apartment hunting.

Stupid panic attack.

Stupid irrational thoughts.

She should just go back to the motel, maybe pick up a newspaper on the way. Surely she could find a decent apartment advertised in the *Statesman*—something that rented by the week or the month, instead of the year.

Yet the idea of going back to an empty room didn't excite her—especially not when her brain was in this much turmoil. No, better to see Matt now and find out what—if anything—was going on. She'd never been very good at shoving things under the rug, anyway.

As she climbed out of the car and headed up the walkway to Matt's house, she felt more like herself than she had since the stupid little wand had turned blue.

WHEN THE DOORBELL RANG, Matt growled at the interruption, then promptly ignored it. He'd had a killer day at work—they'd found out yesterday that they'd landed the Makati project, but that the executives wanted a number of fairly extensive changes to the internal design. And they wanted them two weeks ago. A construction crew had already been lined up and initial permits needed to be obtained—as soon as humanly possible.

Which meant that he and Reece had busted their asses for nearly twelve hours today—and yesterday—to try to give the clients what they wanted, but parts of the building just weren't coming together. Giving the Makati Corporation what they wanted inside meant altering parts of the outside design, and that changed the aesthetics significantly. So significantly that he was having a hard time getting the balance back.

But he didn't want to think about work now, didn't want to think about anything. All he wanted was to veg out in front of his fifty-six-inch flat-screen TV and watch as UT kicked the hell out of University of Oklahoma in baseball. At some point, he'd have to call Camille and check in on her, but not right now. Not yet.

The doorbell rang a second time, and his sense of responsibility wouldn't let him ignore it any longer— what if one of his neighbors had a problem? Muttering a curse, he pushed to his feet and found himself hoping it was one of the solicitors that went door to door in the neighborhood—just so he could kick the intruder off his front porch.

Pulling the door open with a snarl, he stopped dead when he realized Camille was on the other side—looking paler and more distraught than he'd ever seen her.

"What's wrong?" he demanded, as an unfamiliar fear gripped him. "The baby—"

"The baby's fine." She sounded unimpressed with his concern.

"Oh." He stepped aside to let her in. "Okay."

In the other room, he heard the crowd go crazy as the announcer jubilantly screamed about a home run for UT. He clenched his jaw and looked at Camille expectantly.

When she didn't do—or say—anything, he prompted, "Did we have plans?" Then inched his way toward the large great room where his sofa and state-of-the-art entertainment center resided.

"No, I just—" She paused, blew out a breath. "I didn't want to be alone."

With those six words, the game he'd been anticipating all week became just so much background noise. Wrapping an arm around Camille's shoulders, he pulled her against him. "Hey, what's going on? You're not alone."

She gave him a watery smile and alarms went off in his brain. He'd never seen Camille cry, hadn't even been sure she knew how to. Whenever she was around him, she always looked invincible and this sudden change in demeanor had his palms sweating.

"What's wrong? Are you in pain?" He pulled away just far enough to look her over from head to toe, hoping to find something, anything, that might give him a clue to her unusual mood.

"I don't know. I'm just—" A soft, shuddering sob cut off the rest of her words. "Stupid hormones. I've cried more in the past two weeks than I have in the past two years."

He could believe it—one time seemed like more to him. "Come on in, sit down. Do you want some water or apple juice? Maybe some milk?" He'd stocked up with pregnancy-friendly food at the grocery store the other day—before the Makati project had gone to hell in a handbasket.

She laughed as she perched on the edge of the couch, but the sound was tinged with bitterness. "The last time I was in your house and you offered me a drink, I think it was a pomegranate martini. Amazing how a few months change everything."

"Uh, yeah." Matt shoved his hands into the back pockets of his jeans and watched her warily. He was suddenly uncomfortably aware of what it must be like to try to find a path through a minefield. As he searched for something to say that wouldn't set Camille off, more than his palms were damp.

Why the hell didn't pregnant women come with instruction manuals? He'd bet a month's salary that if some poor bastard was brave enough to write one—after surviving an actual pregnancy unscathed—he'd be rich beyond his wildest dreams.

Of course, maybe the reason there was no book was because no man had actually succeeded in coming out the other side without battle wounds. He cleared his throat. Suddenly a pomegranate martini wasn't sounding too bad, even if it was a chick drink.

"Is that a no to the apple juice, then?"

"I don't need anything."

"Okay." He picked up the controller, shut off the TV just as OU had the bases loaded and their strongest hitter was on his way up to bat. He reached for Camille's hand, held it. And tried to ignore the electricity that zinged through him from the contact.

Just friends, he reminded himself. They were just friends now. "So, do you want to talk?"

"Not really. I'm just being stupid."

"So what? It's not like the whole world is sitting here, waiting for your admission."

Her laugh was watery, but at least it was genuine. "Just you."

"Exactly. And before this is over, I have a feeling I'm going to see you in a lot more compromising positions than this."

"Ugh, don't remind me. Labor is definitely not something I'm looking forward to."

Neither was he, but why bring that up when she already looked strung out?

"So, come on. Spit it out."

She shook her head, but when she leaned back against the couch her eyes were dry and she looked much more like the Camille he'd known—or thought he'd known.

He shut the thought down before it could take hold, before he could remember how suicidally stupid it was to want to let her back into his life—even on a platonic basis. After all, it wasn't like he had a choice.

"I'm an idiot. I've got canvas and other supplies that need to be shipped from Italy in the next few days—before my friend who's been holding them for me leaves for Paris—and I can't very well store them in my motel room. So I started looking for an apartment, something up here in North Austin so that you wouldn't have to drive very far to see the baby when…" She cleared her throat.

"Anyway, they wanted me to sign a year's lease and I kind of freaked out."

He'd just bet that she had. For a woman who refused to buy a twelve-pack of soda because it implied too much of a commitment, a yearlong lease had probably sounded like a death knell.

"You know, even though you sign a year's lease, that doesn't mean you have to stay there for a year. The worst that will happen if you leave early is you forfeit the deposit."

"I know that."

"So what's the big deal? If you're concerned about the money—"

He bit his tongue as she shot him a withering look. "It's *not* the money."

"Okay. Of course not." So what the hell was it, then? If she wasn't worried about being locked into a lease without escape and she wasn't freaking out about her deposit, then why—

"It just got me thinking, that's all."

He could relate to that—he'd been doing an awful lot of thinking himself these past few days. And freaking himself out a little more with each new idea that occurred to him.

Now didn't seem the prudent time to bring that up, however.

"The baby won't be born for six months, and then, I assume, I'll have to stick around for a while after the birth, right?"

His heart plummeted to his feet at the implication that she would, indeed, be leaving—sooner rather than later—and taking his child with her. Not that he hadn't expected to have this discussion, but he'd figured he had more time before they got into the fact that he didn't want her to leave.

Correction, didn't want her to take the baby away, he clarified. He refused to have feelings for Camille anymore, at least not beyond her role as the mother of his child. But the baby, that was another matter entirely. Already, he could see himself holding a little girl like Reece's daughter, Rose, or playing catch with a rambunctious little boy, like Reece's twin stepsons.

But another look at Camille's face convinced him that his initial assessment had been right—now wasn't the time for that fight. "I think that's probably wise. A newborn has a lot of needs. A one-week checkup, a two-week checkup, a two-months checkup. Not to mention trying to get everything right with the feeding schedule. And if he or she has jaundice and—" He broke off at her incredulous look.

"What? How do you know all that?"

He shrugged, then gestured to the pile of books sitting on the bookshelf at the other end of the room. "I've been reading about it."

Her laugh, when it came, was much easier this time around. "Of course you have." She pushed off the sofa and crossed to the bookshelf.

Picking up the first book, she read the title. *"What to Expect the First Year."* She put it to the side and looked at the second book. *"How to Have a Smarter Baby."* She sent him an arch look.

"There's nothing wrong with being prepared—" She held up a finger to cut him off, then plowed through the rest of the stack. *"Your Baby and You. The First Six Months. What to Expect When You're Expecting?"* She cracked up at the title of the last book and he could feel his cheeks burning, especially when she started flipping through the book.

"So, Matt, what does the book say you should do about those swollen ankles?"

He cleared his throat, tried for dignified. "I bought that one for you."

"Sure. That's what they all say." But she didn't seem in any hurry to put the book down, flipping through the pages with a mixture of reverence and revulsion. He would have left her to it, except her hands were shaking.

Crossing to her, he pulled the text from Camille's reluctant clutches, then guided her back to the couch with an arm around her waist. "You don't have to have it all figured out today, you know." He repeated the advice Reece had given him a couple of days before. "We have time."

"I know that. I do," she insisted at his skeptical look. "But at the same time, I want to know what's going to happen. I want to make sure I'm prepared."

"You?" he asked with a raised eyebrow. "The woman who won't make a date more than two days in the future because she doesn't know where she'll be any further in advance? The one who picks her next destination by closing her eyes and pointing at a world map?"

She shoved away from him, rolled her eyes in a way he still found strangely endearing—even after everything that had passed between them. "This is different.

This is about my baby. Our baby," she corrected herself. "I don't want to make a mistake that might hurt her or him."

Deep inside him, the core of ice that had been there since she'd walked out on him for Carnaval started to thaw. It didn't melt completely—he was too smart to let that happen—but it warmed up just a little. Camille did care about this baby, did care about doing things the right way. That alone would make things between them so much easier.

"Then don't rush things. It takes time to make a good plan, one that makes sense and points you in the right direction. We'll figure it out."

She smirked. "Don't you mean, you'll figure it out?"

Maybe that was what he meant, but he wasn't stupid enough to say it out loud—at least not to a woman whose emotions were bouncing around like a frog on amphetamines.

At that minute the doorbell rang and he breathed a huge sigh of relief—saved by the bell. "Why don't we start with feeding you? I think that's the pizza I ordered."

Her face lit up like the sun. "You ordered pizza? What kind? Please tell me it's supreme."

"Is there any other kind?"

"Exactly!" She stood up eagerly. "Go get it and I'll grab some plates from the kitchen. Do you want a beer?"

"Yeah. And there's some milk in there—"

"I am *not* drinking milk with pizza. Surely you've got a soft drink in there, somewhere." She disappeared into his kitchen.

He smiled as he went to answer the door. He'd picked up some Sprite when he'd stopped for gas the night before—figuring he'd need it if Camille stopped by. And he'd been right. No matter what Reece said, there was merit in having a well thought-out plan, one that provided for unexpected contingencies.

CHAPTER SEVEN

THEY ATE PIZZA AND SALAD—Matt had insisted on making one because she and the baby needed vitamins—on the family-room floor, while Texas creamed Oklahoma on the huge flat-screen TV. They talked of stupid things—the weather, a musician they both liked, the game—and laughed a lot, though later Camille wouldn't have been able to say what they'd both found so funny.

For the first time since she'd returned to Austin, things were easy between them. Relaxed. And she couldn't help remembering why she'd fallen for Matt in the first place—and why she'd been tempted to break her own rules with him all those months before.

In the dim light of the TV, she couldn't see Matt's eyes clearly, but his mouth was stretched in a sexy grin— one that had her heart pounding just a little too fast and her toes tingling in a way that would probably end up spelling disaster. But in those moments of friendly intimacy, she couldn't bring herself to care. The pizza was delicious, the company even more so, and she found herself relaxing despite the stress and fear that had sent her running over to Matt's in the first place.

And she wasn't even going to touch that right now—the fact that she'd instinctively gone to him for comfort. Nor was she going to focus on the fact that he had, indeed, comforted her.

In the grand scheme of things, what was a security deposit, after all?

"Do you want the last piece?" Matt held it up enticingly.

"Are you kidding? I'm so full I might explode."

"Don't do that—I've also got butter pecan ice cream in the freezer."

She groaned. "Now, that's not right. You know it's my favorite."

"I do, indeed."

"So, you are trying to kill me?"

"Nope, just fatten you up a little bit."

"Nice." She shot him a mock glare. "There is such a thing as being too honest."

He grinned. "I've heard that somewhere before."

"You just don't believe in it?"

"I never said that. I grew up in a house with four women—believe me, I know the merits of a well-placed 'No, of course that doesn't make your butt look big.' Probably a lot better than most guys."

"What was that like?"

"Lying to my sisters? Self-preservation, mostly. Fun, other times."

"No, I meant growing up in a big family." She gestured to the fireplace mantel, where he had a number of family pictures clustered. "Was it difficult?"

He started to give her the same pat answer he gave everyone, but she wasn't everyone—and never would be. In the end, he settled for the truth. "Sometimes. My dad ran out on my mom when she was pregnant with my youngest sisters and we never saw him again."

"I'm so sorry. That must have been—"

He shook his head. "Don't be sorry. It wasn't as bad as everyone thought. We were lucky—my mom was one of those women who'd gone to college and had a good job even thirty years ago, so it's not like she had no options. Plus, Dad was always pretty decent about sending money. Not a lot, and not regularly, but a few times a year a check would show up—usually around Christmas or our birthdays, when Mom really needed the extra cash. That was back in the days before deadbeat dads were taken to task."

"He did that, but he never came back to see you? Or her?"

"No." He shrugged. "But like I said, we did okay. My oldest sister, Rhiannon, was three and a half years older than me and nine years older than the twins, so she was always stuck with babysitting the three of us. It probably sucked for her, but she never complained."

"I bet it wasn't so bad. You were probably a really responsible kid."

He laughed. "I was a holy terror, and so were the twins. We were always in trouble."

"Really?" She looked fascinated. "You're such a stand-up guy I have trouble imagining you doing anything that terrible."

"Oh, you'd be surprised. I got into more than my fair share of trouble."

"Like what?"

He thought for a minute. "I spray painted my sister's cat once. Electric-green."

"You did not!"

"I did. I also stole the neighbor's goat and hid it in my bathtub, put lizards in my sisters' beds and dyed Rhiannon and her first boyfriend blue by putting a ton of food coloring in the hot tub."

"Blue?"

He nodded. "Oh, yeah."

"Why blue?"

"It was the same color as the lining of the hot tub. They couldn't see it—until they got out, and by then it was too late."

She stared at him, amazed. "You were diabolical."

"I was—absolutely."

"So what happened? You just grew out of it?"

"Something like that."

"Something like what?"

"Life has a way of coming full circle, you know?" For a fleeting moment he thought of his childhood— of the day his youngest sister had gone missing when he was supposed to be watching her—then let the old, painful memory go. She had been found, but the hours they had spent searching were among the worst of his life. Still, if he'd learned one thing in his life, it was that dwelling on the past got him nowhere. Concentrating on the future—planning for it—was the way to go.

A little upset at how much he'd revealed, he glanced over at Camille, who was watching him with a rare understanding in her eyes. Usually he felt as if they were worlds apart, but in that moment, it seemed she understood everything he *hadn't* said. Instead of making him uncomfortable, it made him feel good, as if there was something more between them than the baby.

Maybe that was why he gave voice to the idea that had been circling in his head since she'd come to his door, upset about the twelve-month lease. "Move in with me."

For long seconds, Camille didn't move, didn't react at all—almost as if she hadn't heard him. Not that he blamed her—the idea had come out of nowhere. Still, it felt right, so he prepared to voice the request again, a little more delicately this time. But just as he opened his mouth, she whispered, "What did you say?"

"I want you to move in with me," he repeated. "It's the perfect solution."

"For who?"

"For both of us. For all three of us."

"What are you talking about?" She stared at him in disbelief. "Where did this come from?"

"I've been thinking about it since you got here."

"Wow, a whole hour and a half. You've really thought this out then, huh, Matt?"

"How much thought do I need to put into it to know the idea makes sense?"

"And I thought I was the impulsive one in this relationship. You're talking about changing our entire lives, yet you give more thought to where you want to go to dinner than you've given this whole idea."

"Maybe," he answered, though he knew she was right. Normally he would have sweated over the decision, thought about it for days or weeks. But he didn't have weeks—odds were Camille would settle on an apartment in the next few days if he didn't convince her to move in with him.

And suddenly, it really did seem like the best solution. The only solution. If they were living apart, he would miss out on whole chunks of his child's life—like his father had. And while he'd never truly felt deprived growing up without a father, there were times through the years that he'd really wished his dad had been there.

He didn't want his own child going through that. He wanted—needed—to be there for him or her. The thought had him pushing at her to agree with him.

"Come on, Camille. Think about it. Any decent apartment you look at is going to require a twelve-month lease. That's pretty standard stuff here in Austin. If you move in here, you won't have to worry about a lease at all. And you'll have me around to help with the baby."

"The baby's not due for six months."

"Pregnancy stuff, then. You'll need help as you get further along—you can't do it all alone and I'm more than capable of giving you whatever help you need."

As soon as the words were out of his mouth, he knew he'd said the wrong thing. Camille had stiffened, her eyes turning frigid. Her next words confirmed his suspicions. "I'm a big girl, Matt. I don't need you—or anyone—to take care of me."

He started to backpedal. "I didn't mean it like that."

Her smile was so sharp that he felt it slice into him. "You said I should move in here so you can *help* me—with the baby, with pregnancy stuff. That you could do things for me that I can't do on my own. How else am I supposed to take it?"

"I only meant that I could make things easier for you. My friend's wife had to go through a pregnancy alone—it's not a picnic." He felt his own temper start to rise. "I'm just trying to help, Camille. Can't you cut me some slack?"

"There's that word again. *Help*." She threw her paper plate into the empty pizza box before pushing to her feet. "I'm not a charity case, Matt. I haven't asked you for a damn thing."

"And you won't. I get that. No matter how much it frustrates me, I do get that." He stood, followed her across the room to where she was standing, hands on hips. "But does that mean I can't offer?"

"I don't know! I don't know anything anymore. Two weeks ago I was in Italy looking at centuries-old architecture, studying paintings done by the Masters, with nothing more pressing on my mind than what museum I should visit that day or what I should paint next.

"Then, suddenly, I'm pregnant and my whole life has changed. I've been on my own since I was seventeen years old, never answering to anyone. And suddenly here you are, expecting me to answer to you. Telling me how much to eat and when to sleep and what I can or cannot paint with. Now you're even telling me where to live."

"No. That's not it at all." He stared at her incredulously, shocked at how wrong she'd gotten it. He'd only been trying to— He cut himself off before he could so much as think the word that she'd found so offensive. "I just want to be involved."

"Don't you mean you just want to be in control?"

It was his turn to walk away as fury pounded through him. What the hell was wrong with her? Most women wanted their baby's fathers to take an interest, to be involved. Yet Camille viewed everything he did as an attack. As some kind of power trip. How was he supposed to convince her otherwise? And why the hell should he have to? She was the one who had twisted him into knots over her and then just walked away. So why was he suddenly the one who had to prove himself to her?

CAMILLE WATCHED AS MATT clenched and unclenched his fists. There was temper in the sharp line of his spine, in his taut jaw and curled fingers. A small part of her— one that she'd thought she'd buried long before—was afraid that he would take that anger out on her, and that only made her more upset. More confused. Matt was the most gentle, controlled man she'd ever met and yet he looked on the verge of punching a hole through the wall. Because of her. Because she'd dared to disagree with him.

For a minute, memories of her mother, of her father— of everything they'd put each other through—rose up from the dead and haunted her. But she pushed them back, pushed it all back, into the tidy compartment at the back of her mind. And tried to see the situation from Matt's point of view.

It wasn't easy when she'd felt as if he'd been telling her what to do from the moment he'd shown up at her motel room door.

"Look, Matt, I'm sorry if I misread your intentions. I just feel like you've been pushing at me since I told you about the baby and I don't like to be pushed. I'm not ready to make decisions yet."

She saw his shoulders rise and fall as he took one deep breath after another. Silence stretched between them, long seconds ticking by as Matt tried to rein in his temper. It must have worked, because when he turned to face her she couldn't find any sign of the anger that had all but set the room on fire a few minutes before.

His eyes were clear and his voice steady as he answered, "That's why I thought moving in here would be perfect for you. If it works out, great. If it doesn't, then you can move out—no harm, no foul. But it gives you time to breathe, time you don't necessarily have sitting in a motel room."

She studied him, saw nothing but sincerity in his expression, and let herself relax, just a little bit. What he was saying made sense, to a degree. But at the same time, she couldn't help feeling a little like Alice after she'd fallen down the rabbit hole.

Move in with Matt? Be exposed to all that smoldering sensuality every day of her life? Some women didn't find competence sexy—hell, she'd always considered herself one of those women—but there was something to be said for feeling taken care of. Cherished. Matt was a decent guy in every sense and she was beginning to believe that she could rely on him to be there for her, no matter what.

Not that she needed him, she assured herself as she gathered up the pizza box and assorted other trash and carried it into the kitchen. She didn't need anyone to take care of her—she never had.

But still, it would be nice not to have to sweat the details.

To not have to apartment hunt.

To just go with the flow, for once, instead of always swimming upstream—just to prove that she could.

It wasn't like moving in with Matt would exactly be a hardship. He had a lovely house, with a great big loft upstairs that had fantastic light. It would be ideal for her painting, and though he currently used it for his own office, she was sure she could get him to share. She'd always had better than average persuasive skills and he was generous to a fault—or at least he had been, before she'd left three months before. And nothing he'd done in the past few days had shown her any differently.

As she walked back into the living room, she was incredibly conscious of Matt beside her. He was only a few feet away and the urge to go to him, to ask him to hold her for a minute, was nearly overwhelming. A few months ago she would have done it without thinking twice—but then, a few months ago it wouldn't have meant anything.

Not that it would mean anything now, she reminded herself. Not to Matt, who was determined to keep things on an even footing. And not to her. For years, she'd used sex to keep men she cared about at a distance—it was so much easier to concentrate on physical sensations instead of her true emotions. And for years it had worked.

Yet even as she reassured herself of that fact, she couldn't help wondering if it was still true. She'd thought the wild, crazy sex she'd had with Matt three months before had helped keep things from getting serious between them, but now she wasn't so sure. There was a connection between them—even after all these weeks— that had nothing to do with the baby inside her. Suddenly she was having a terrible time holding on to her usual sense of distance. If they were to add sex back into the equation… Would it help her regain her perspective or make her lose it completely?

She couldn't take the risk—not when her feelings for Matt were so complicated. And not when she had a baby to think about.

No, it was better to remain friends only. *Platonic* friends who just happened to share a baby. Her traitorous mind went back to the kiss in his car a few days before and Camille could feel herself flush. But she refused to give in to it. One minor setback did not a relationship define.

"You know," she said as she crossed to him, making sure to keep her hands firmly in her pockets. "You can still have a role in the pregnancy without giving up your home to me, Matt."

"I know that, but it wouldn't be the same. I wouldn't be there for all the little things—"

"What little things? You're the father—no offense, but you really don't have that much to do for the next six months. Especially since we're not—you know—together."

His eyes narrowed. "What would I do differently if we were—you know—together?" He mimicked her words.

"I don't know." She looked over his shoulder at the television, pretended an interest in the crowd he knew she didn't give a damn about. "It's not like I've done this before."

"Exactly! Neither of us has done this before, so who cares what we're supposed to do? Or what other people do? Or what my role is supposed to be? It's not like either of us has ever been big on convention."

Her look was skeptical. "And you think my moving in with you is a good precedent for us to set?"

"Absolutely—it solves your problem of where to live. You can come and go as you please, and if you decide you want to take off for a while—" he nearly choked on the words, on the idea of her taking off with his child inside her, but somehow managed to continue "—then that's fine, too. You don't have to worry about what to do with the baby stuff or how to juggle your lease or any of the other problems. You can just go."

"And, I assume, come back."

"Well, yes. I mean, I will have visitation rights, won't I?"

She sighed, shocked at how much his uncertainty hurt her—especially since he had every right to his distrust. "That's not even an issue, Matt. I think we're both adult enough to deal with that side of things."

"I'm glad."

He didn't say anything else, didn't try to pressure her to see his point of view, and that, more than anything else, convinced her to take a leap of faith.

"So, if I decided to move in, where would I stay?" she asked.

Matt's sudden smile was so wide that it made her heart skip a beat—or three. "I've got two guest rooms— you can take whichever one you want."

"And where would I work?"

He snorted. "You already know the answer to that. You've been lusting after my office for months."

"You'll clear out space for my canvasses?"

"I'll let you have the whole thing—one of the guest rooms has pretty good light. I can make it my office for the time being."

Was she really thinking about doing this? she wondered a little frantically. Was she really going to commit to— *No harm, no foul.* Matt's words came back to her, calmed her down as nothing else could have at that point. This didn't have to be permanent. It wasn't permanent. It was just for a while, until the baby was born. Until she knew what she wanted to do next.

"I guess I only have one question then."

"Which is?"

"How much rent do you charge?"

CHAPTER EIGHT

"WHAT ARE YOU STOCKING UP for, World War Three?" Camille asked a few weeks later as Matt loaded their grocery cart with three different types of apples.

"I've got a busy week ahead—I don't have time to come back here." He dropped two heads of broccoli in a bag, then laid them gently on top of the apples.

"Yes, but I happen to have an almost completely open schedule this week—I can stop in and pick something up anytime."

"Why would you want to?" he asked as he headed toward the dairy section. "It's easier to just get whatever we need for the week in one trip."

"But how do you know what you're in the mood for all week? What if I suddenly get a craving for fettuccine Alfredo on Thursday and all we've got is chicken and broccoli?"

He looked at her sharply. "Are you craving fettuccini?"

"No. That was just an example."

"Are you sure?" He wheeled down the pasta aisle, pulled a box of the thick pasta off the shelf. "Because we can get some—"

"Matt, you're missing the whole point." She let out a disgusted sigh.

"No, I'm not. You don't want to be tied down, even to something as basic as chicken on Thursday night."

"It's not about being tied down—it's about not knowing what I'll be in the mood for."

"It's about the fact that you can't commit to anything more than forty-eight hours in the future."

"I've committed to having this baby, haven't I? And to living with you."

"Yeah, but for how long?" Matt smirked at her, and though his tone said he was clearly teasing, the look in his eyes had an edge of seriousness that made her uncomfortable.

"You don't really worry about that, do you? Me walking out?"

"Come on, Camille. Let's just get the shopping done."

"No." She reached out, put a hand on his arm and felt the familiar zing as his energy rushed through her. When was she going to get used to it? To him? They'd been living together for almost a month and he still curled her toes whenever he looked at her. "I want to talk about this."

He glanced around the busy supermarket. "Not now."

"Why not now? If you're really concerned—"

"Concerned? Shopping more than forty-eight hours in advance is too much commitment for you. Why wouldn't I worry about you getting bored and taking off on me?"

She stopped dead in the middle of the aisle, tried to assimilate his words. "I wouldn't do that, just take—" She paused in midsentence as Matt skewered her with a patently disbelieving look. And she guessed she couldn't blame him. She had left him high and dry once before—was it any wonder he thought she'd do it again?

But this was different. She was happy living with Matt, happy with the commissions she'd picked up to do portraits instead of having to struggle to sell her art on the streets of each brand-new city. Her restless feet had lost their urge to run, and though she didn't know how long it would last—surely she'd get the itch to move on sometime—for once she was in no hurry.

It took her a minute to sort her thoughts out and by the time she worked herself around to what she wanted to say, Matt had already turned the corner on the next aisle and she was forced to rush to keep up with him.

That made her uncomfortable; Matt's penchant for taking the lead was too reminiscent of her parents' relationship for her to brush it off. She'd spent her whole adult life blazing new trails and she resented the fact that Matt expected her to follow him blindly, even as he was insulting her. She wasn't some meek little housewife to follow behind her man, no matter what he said or did.

She watched as he turned along yet another aisle, not even glancing behind him to see if she was following, and the little itch between her shoulder blades ratcheted up a notch. Turning on her heel, she walked in the opposite direction, toward the store entrance, and then out the big, sliding glass doors at the front of the building. If she remembered correctly, there was a little jewelry and handbag place over to the right....

Camille spent the next few minutes browsing through purses and earrings, two of her favorite things. Though she only owned one bag—how many could she carry, after all?—she'd had a love affair with earrings since she was a kid. She had a train case full of the dangly, sparkly things.

Her cell phone rang as she was holding a pair of bright red chandelier earrings up to her ear, trying to get an idea of how they would look. For a second, she contemplated letting it ring, but figured there was no need to be bitchy. Surely, she'd made her point.

Fishing the small, purple phone out of her bag, she wasn't the least surprised to see Matt's number on the caller ID.

"Hello?"

"Where are you? I've searched the entire store for you."

"I'm next door, at the accessory store."

There was a long silence. "You're where?"

She made sure there was a shrug in her voice when she answered, "You didn't seem to need me, not the way you were blazing trails up and down the aisles."

"You couldn't tell me you were leaving?"

"I would have had to run to catch up with you."

"And God forbid you should do that, right? Camille Arraby doesn't chase after any man."

His voice was ripe with annoyance, but there was something else there—something she couldn't quite put her finger on. But it made her feel guilty for leaving, even though he'd been the one behaving like an ass. The guilt didn't sit well, so she found herself resorting to the flippant answers she'd used for years, to keep people—and emotions—at bay.

"Aww, don't get your panties in a wad, sweets. It's nothing personal."

"Believe me, I never thought it was." He paused, and she could almost see him running a hand through his hair as he struggled for control. What would it be like, she wondered, if he ever really let go? If he ever just did what his instincts told him to without trying to temper it with logic first?

"I'm going to check out. I should be at the car in about five minutes—is that enough time for you to look for accessories or do you need a few more minutes?" His voice was level, even, calm, and if she hadn't been listening closely, she never would have heard the sarcasm in his words. But she did hear it, this time, and couldn't help wondering what else she'd missed these past few weeks.

The uncertainty was enough to make her tone down her own attitude. "I'll meet you at the car."

"Fine." He clicked off without another word and she slowly let out the breath she hadn't known she was holding.

She put the earrings back on the shelf where she'd found them, then slowly worked her way toward the front door of the shop—killing time as she waited for Matt to finish. Even though she knew it was stupid, she refused to be sitting by the car, waiting for him, like some recalcitrant schoolchild. She didn't have that much give in her.

By the time she got to the car, Matt was already there, loading the trunk. She reached for a bag, started to help him, but he snatched it away before she could pick it up. "That one's heavy."

"I'm not an invalid, Matt."

"I never said you were, but why lift heavy stuff if you don't have to?"

She reached for another bag, this one filled with whole wheat bread and bagels, and waited for him to say something about it being too heavy, as well. He didn't, just kept loading the other bags, so she placed the bread carefully in the trunk then made her way around to the passenger seat.

Her disappearing act had obviously made her point— and she'd upset Matt as much as he'd upset her. Why then did her victory feel so hollow?

Matt didn't say a word when he climbed into the car, and the trip home was one of the most uncomfortable of her life, the tension in the air so thick she could feel it.

Should she apologize, she wondered, tell him that taking off had been a stupid thing to do? But he was the one who'd been leveling barbs at her, and left her standing in the middle of the grocery store, even as she tried to talk to him. Shouldn't he apologize first?

Ugh. This was so why she didn't do relationships. All this jockeying for position, trying to decide all the time who was right and who was wrong. It was irritating and stressful and took far more energy than the stupid relationship was usually worth.

Matt pulled into the garage and she was out of the car before he'd so much as put the thing in Park. If he didn't want her help carrying bags, then fine, he could do it all himself. She had better things to do than to put away a month's worth of groceries, anyway.

She made her way up to her studio, but as she heard Matt bringing in the bags—he was always the responsible one—guilt assailed her. She hadn't paid for her half of the groceries and now she was acting like a child, leaving him to do everything on his own.

With a sigh, she decided it didn't matter who was right or wrong in their stupid fight—she couldn't keep acting like a witch all night because of it.

Reaching into her purse, she pulled out her wallet and made her way to the kitchen. Matt was in the garage, gathering up more bags, as she started to put the fresh produce away in the refrigerator.

"I can do that," he said on his final trip into the kitchen, then closed and locked the garage door behind him.

"I can help—I assume all this green stuff is for me, after all." She shot him a little smile, but he wasn't looking at her.

About halfway through putting the groceries away she ran across the receipt. Reaching into her wallet, she pulled out sixty dollars and laid it on the counter. "Here's my half of the grocery money."

She hadn't thought it possible, but Matt's spine stiffened even more. For a minute, she thought he was finally going to let loose with whatever was inside him, but he just clenched his jaw and continued to load the pantry.

She was about to give up—it was impossible to have a conversation with a man who wouldn't speak to you—when he asked, "Do you regret it?"

Her eyes shot to his. "Regret what? Leaving you in the grocery store?"

"The baby. And coming back here, telling me about it."

She started to give him some silly little nonanswer, the kind she used whenever a question hit too close to home. But he was finally reaching out, and he looked so intense, so vulnerable, that she couldn't force herself to brush him off.

Clasping her hands in front of herself, she looked at them instead of him as she answered, "*Regret* isn't the right word."

"So what *is* the right word?" When she paused, he added, "Don't worry about hurting my feelings or making me angry, Camille. I really want to know what's going on inside of you."

"I don't *know* what's going on inside of me right now."

His mouth tightened. "That's a cop-out answer."

"No, it's an honest one. A cop-out answer would be me telling you that everything is fine when it clearly isn't.

"I'm confused and worried and nervous and happy and...ugh. There are so many emotions inside of me right now that it's nearly impossible for me to sort them all out, let alone explain them to you."

"I'm glad I'm not the only one."

The idea of Matt being nervous was so patently absurd that she started to laugh. But the sound died in her throat as she realized he wasn't joining her. He was being honest with her, letting her see behind the cool, competent facade he wore so well. It was the first real glimpse behind the mask he'd worn since she'd walked out on him for Carnaval.

"What are you nervous about?"

"A better question would be what am I not nervous about. I'm worried about your pregnancy and the chemicals in the paint you use affecting the baby. About what will happen after he or she is born. About how we'll work things out between us. About how much I'll miss the baby when you take off on your next jaunt around the world. About how many hours I work and how that will affect my relationship with…" His voice trailed off abruptly and she didn't fill the silence. She couldn't think of anything to say.

"Why'd you take off in the supermarket?" The question came out of left field, considering what they'd been talking about, but she answered it as honestly as she could.

"You made me angry, the way you just walked away from me in the middle of a conversation." As if what she'd had to say wasn't even worth hanging around and listening to.

"I wasn't walking away from you. I was just trying to get my own thoughts in order. Being around you isn't exactly conducive to my thinking straight."

It was the nicest thing anyone had ever said to her, and despite every word of caution she'd given herself since her return, Camille didn't even try to check the impulse to touch him. With a soft smile that she hadn't even known she had in her, she ran a hand through his silky hair. Let her thumb linger on the sharp stubble of his cheek. Gave her fingers permission to toy with the nape of his neck.

It was strange to think of Matt as being confused. He was always the one in control, always the one with the answer, and to find out that he was as anxious and worried and messed up inside as she was, warmed her in a way she didn't understand. She didn't like that he was suffering, but it was nice to know she wasn't in this alone. That she wasn't a screwup for not knowing what to do.

Leaning forward, she brushed her lips over his right cheek, then his left. She started to pull away, but Matt's hands came up and cupped her face, his thumbs stroking softly over her own cheekbones. He moved slowly, giving her a chance to pull away if she wanted to.

She didn't want to. Her heart was beating like a metronome on high speed and her breathing was shallow, but she didn't so much as move—afraid he would take it as a rejection.

When she didn't protest, he inched closer, his mouth hovering so close to hers that she could feel his every exhalation. She could smell the spicy cinnamon of the gum he usually chewed, could sense his reluctance and his need.

And when his lips finally closed over hers, she could taste the sweet and sexy heat of him.

He kissed her slowly, carefully, as if afraid to startle her. His lips were soft as they nibbled on hers, his tongue warm and honeyed as it stroked over her lips, asking for entrance.

She let him in with a sigh, then shivered as he swept inside. His tongue explored her thoroughly, leisurely, tracing her lips, the roof of her mouth, her teeth, before tangling with her own.

She whimpered deep in her throat, and he started to pull away. But she reached up, tangled her hands in his hair, held him close to her. And the world exploded—fire and need and tenderness arcing between them.

His mouth grew harder, more aggressive, and his hands tightened on her shoulders, pulled her closer until her body was flush with his. And still he kissed her, with a single-minded determination that made her feel like the sexiest woman in the world.

But when she was fully aroused, was moaning and clawing at him, her hips bumping his in her determination to get closer, Matt pulled away.

They stared at each other in the rapidly darkening kitchen, mouths swollen and chests heaving with the effort to pull air into oxygen-deprived lungs. Turned on, frustrated, more needy than she could ever remember being, she reached for him.

He shook his head, backed away. Left her standing in the kitchen staring after him, her body aroused and her spirit crushed.

MATT WALKED AWAY FROM Camille without a backward glance, afraid to trust himself to even look at her. One word from her and he'd be back in the kitchen, bending her over a chair and taking her the way he'd been fantasizing about for weeks—for months—now.

Slamming into his bedroom, his control shot to hell and back, he braced his hands on his dresser and asked himself what he was doing.

She'd walked out on him at the grocery store without so much as a word and here he was, less than an hour later, contemplating making love to her on his kitchen table. Where was his control? Where was his *pride?*

The same place it had always been when it came to Camille—gone as if it had never been.

What had he been thinking moving her in here? Letting her back into his life? Had he really been so naive, so stupid, as to think he could keep his hands off her? Sure, he'd succeeded, but every day was torture. He'd taken more cold showers in the past month than he had during his entire teenage years, and that was saying something. And now, this. Kissing her when he should be doing anything but. Nearly taking her when he should be distancing himself from her in a big way.

So what the hell was he doing?

It was a question he still didn't have an answer for the next day, when he met his oldest sister for lunch.

"I want to meet her."

"Who?" Matt asked, starting guiltily as Rhiannon raised one perfect eyebrow at him. Though Camille had been back in his life for more than a month, he hadn't told Rhiannon about her yet. He'd told himself it was because his sister had enough to deal with—her husband of twelve years had walked out after the man who had attacked her the year before had failed to be convicted—and he hadn't wanted to add more to her load. But as he stared into her knowing eyes, he realized the truth was more complicated—and more simple.

He hadn't wanted her to look at him in just that way, to ask for answers he didn't have.

"The woman who's put the sparkle in your eyes and the snarl on your lips." She leaned closer, smiled in an effort to lessen the harshness of her words. "After the way you fell apart when Camille left, I wasn't sure I'd ever see you interested in another woman."

"I didn't fall apart." He shifted uncomfortably, tried to look anywhere but into his sister's warm, green eyes. "I didn't even miss a day of work."

"Oh, I know. You didn't do it on the outside. But inside you were shattered—I helped raised you, Matt. Do you think I didn't realize how hurt you were? You shut down inside, stopped coming around, stopped calling. You even dodged my calls, staying on the phone only long enough to make sure I was all right."

"I was busy."

"You were heartbroken. Maybe you didn't recognize it, since it's never happened to you before, but that's what you were. Believe me, I recognize the signs."

Right away, he felt like a total heel. Here he was brooding about his own life while his sister was recovering from a brutal rape and the subsequent end of her marriage. The fact that he hadn't been there for her—that he hadn't even known Richard had left until weeks after the fact—was just one more failure on his part. It was his job to take care of her, to take care of all his sisters, and he'd been so wrapped up in his own misery that he'd completely fallen down on the job.

It was just one more reason for him to keep as much distance between himself and Camille as he possibly could.

"Well, I'm better now. So you can stop worrying about me."

Rhiannon laughed. "Yes, because we Jenkinses are so good at that, right? I'll stop worrying about you the same time you stop worrying about me."

Since he didn't have a comeback for that, Matt did the prudent thing and buried his head in the menu. But he couldn't stay hidden forever and when he finally set it aside, it was to find Rhiannon still watching him with an equal mixture of love and exasperation.

"What?" he asked, slumping defensively in his seat.

"You never answered my question."

Knowing he was quickly running out of options—Camille's pregnancy was beginning to show—he bit the bullet and told her, "Camille's back."

Rhiannon didn't say anything for a minute, but then, what could she say? Despite his protests, she'd been dead-on with her earlier assessment. He had fallen apart when Camille had left, had shattered inside when she'd walked out his door, and it had only gotten worse with every phone call she refused to answer.

"Is she planning on sticking around for a while this time?"

The anger in her voice would have made him smile, if her concerns weren't so close to his own. "She's a little over four months pregnant."

"I see. So she came running back to you so that you could fix everything."

He straightened up abruptly. "That's not fair."

"Maybe not. But she hurt you, badly. You'll have to forgive me if I'm skeptical about her sudden change of heart—especially since it comes with a baby attached."

"She hasn't had a change of heart. We're having a baby together, but we're not *together.*"

He did his best to ignore the images of the kiss they'd shared the night before—and the need that was still tying him up in knots.

"And how's that working out for you?" Rhiannon didn't bother to hide her skepticism.

"Okay—for the most part. Considering the fact that she's living with me."

"Are you telling me that your former girlfriend—who ripped your heart out and stomped on it—is back in town, pregnant with your child and living with you?"

"Yeah."

"And you didn't think any of us would want to know about that? Me, the twins, Mom?"

"I've been busy."

"You've been hiding."

"Look, Rhiannon, it's complicated."

"I'm sure it is. So why don't you explain it to me?"

"She's back in town until the baby is born, but after that, it's anyone's guess. She'll probably take off to parts unknown and there isn't much I can do to stop her."

"With the baby, or is she planning on leaving the kid with you?"

"Oh, I'm sure she'll take the baby with her." He nearly choked on the words.

"I can see how well that idea sits with you."

"What do you want me to say? That I'm worried she'll just up and disappear one day? That she won't stick around until the baby's born? That I'll be forced to chase her—and my kid—around the world if I want to have anything to do with it?"

"*Are* you worried?"

"Of course I am. She runs away at the slightest provocation. I feel like I'm walking on eggshells all the time, trying not to say or do anything that will upset her so she won't take off."

"That's got to be wearing on you."

"You have no idea." Last night he'd been tired and annoyed and had snapped at Camille in the grocery store. And how had she responded? By walking out on him without so much as a word. He'd spent fifteen minutes searching the damn store for her, only to find out that she was next door. And Rhiannon wanted to know if it was wearing on him? He was so strung out it was a miracle his hair wasn't standing straight up.

"That's not in your power, you know."

"What?"

"Whether or not Camille stays or goes. You don't control that, can't control it. Only she can."

"I'm well aware of that."

She shook her head. "I don't think you are. From the moment Marissa went missing when you were thirteen, you've tried to control everything. You became the perfect student, the perfect son, the perfect brother, the perfect man. You plan everything, control everything."

"She nearly died—and it was my fault."

"Yes. But she didn't die. She spent two cold, uncomfortable nights lost in the woods and was spoiled rotten when she was found. Marissa barely remembers it, but you—you've let it rule your entire life."

Matt couldn't look his sister in the eye. "She was my responsibility and I let her get lost."

"You've spent the past twenty-two years of your life making up for that fact, trying to protect everyone and everything around you. But some things aren't in your control. *Camille* isn't in your control—nothing you do is going to make her stay if she doesn't want to stay. Believe me, if I've learned nothing else from the past eighteen months, I've learned that."

Rhiannon's words hit like punches, maybe even harder than she'd intended because he recognized the truth in them. However, knowing she was right didn't make what she had to say any easier to swallow.

"You know, I came here to tell you I was going to be a father. Maybe get some congratulations—"

"Congratulations! Of course, I'm excited for you. You'll be a terrific dad, Matt. Absolutely fabulous."

He brushed her words away. "She's carrying my baby, Rhiannon. Am I just supposed to back off and hope for the best? I want to be a part of this child's life. I need to be a part of it."

"Of course you do. I'm not suggesting otherwise."

Maybe not, but she was shaking the whole foundation on which he'd built his life. Just sit back? Let things play out? Don't try to plan for the future or take care of things? He didn't have a clue how to do that, didn't know if he'd want to do it even if he did know how.

When he didn't respond, Rhiannon continued, "This is just my perspective—and keep in mind, I'm on the outside looking in. But it seems to me that the harder you try to hold on to Camille, the more likely you are to lose her."

"I'm not trying to hold on to Camille."

Rhiannon's smile was sad. "Aren't you?"

"Of course not. I know a losing proposition when I see one. But she comes with the baby, so what am I supposed to do?"

"Is that all she is to you? The mother of your child?"

He wanted to say yes, *needed* the answer to be yes. When Camille had shown up on his doorstep five weeks before, he'd promised himself that he wouldn't let her in. Wouldn't give her the chance to hurt him again. Yet here he was, thinking about her, *wanting* her, and a big part of that desire had nothing to do with the baby.

So where did that leave him? he wondered in disgust. On the same course to make the same mistakes with her he'd already made? Expecting her to feel about him the way he felt about her? He'd done that once and had gotten his heart shredded. It was suicide, going down this road again, when he already knew how things were going to turn out. What was his mother's definition of insanity—doing the same thing over and over again, hoping for a different result? Living with Camille, cooking for her, watching movies with her, just *being* with her, had definitely felt familiar. It had also felt right, and that's what really, truly scared the hell out of him. It's what had made him walk away from her in the kitchen last night and it was what had him sitting here, trying to convince his sister that he had everything under control.

How was he supposed to do this again—be sucked into the chaos and confusion and lack of promises that was her life? He was already a part of it—the baby guaranteed that much—but that didn't mean he had to sink all the way back in. Didn't mean he had to give himself up to the insanity.

And yet here he was, thinking about the little dimple at the left corner of Camille's mouth, of her strawberry-and-brown-sugar scent. Of her soft, wild hair and what it felt like to bury his face in it after he'd made love to her.

Clearing his throat, he said with a definitiveness he was far from feeling, "That's all I'll let her be. The mother of my child."

Rhiannon searched his face, then reached one delicate, fine-boned hand across the table to cover his. "You know I'm just worried about you, right? That I want what's best for you because I love you."

"I know." He glanced down and saw the thin, white scars crisscrossing the back of her hand. Though she was wearing long sleeves, he knew the same scars formed a line up both her forearms—defensive wounds from

the brutal attack she'd survived a year and a half ago—
and her words came back to him. He couldn't control
everything, not even close. If he could, she would never
have been hurt. Marissa would never have been lost. And
Camille—Camille would never have left him.

Rhiannon's smile was sad, but her eyes were clear
when she said, "I'm not giving you any advice that I'm
not willing to follow, you know. I met with a real estate
agent last week and the house goes on the market on
Monday."

"Are you sure you want to do that? I can help you
with the payments—"

Rhiannon's hand clapped playfully over his mouth.
"What did I just tell you? You can't fix everything."

"Maybe not. But I can fix this. How much do you
need?"

"I need to fix this, Matt. It's my life and it's important
to me that I do it on my own." She rapidly drained her
cup of coffee.

"Now I have to go. My new boss wants to meet to
discuss the details of an upcoming event."

"On a Saturday?"

"Yes, on a Saturday." She grabbed her purse, leaned
over and kissed him on the cheek. He pulled her into
a hug and held on to the familiar honeysuckle scent of
her, this woman who had partially raised him. "Now,
I hope you don't mind, but I'm sticking you with the
bill." Then, pulling away, she added, "Call me and tell
me what you end up deciding."

As Matt watched his sister walk away, her limp barely
noticeable after two surgeries and extensive physical
therapy, he wondered what he was supposed to do now.

He'd come to lunch hoping his sister could help him clarify his relationship with Camille, but he was more confused than ever.

Give up control?

Trust Camille not to leave him?

Step back as Rhiannon struggled to do things on her own?

Let all the cards around him simply fall where they may?

Just thinking the words made him shudder, but then he didn't know what other choice he had. But in the back of his head, while he paid the check, he couldn't help wondering where all this hands-off behavior left him. In his mind, it didn't bode well when the man who was known for making and sticking with the most detailed of plans couldn't follow his latest one from one minute to the next.

CHAPTER NINE

THREE WEEKS LATER, MATT was still trying to sort things out in his mind. During that time, he'd managed to keep his distance from Camille—which hadn't been all that difficult as she'd alternated between treating him like a casual friend and a plague victim, depending on what the situation called for. Though she was willing to hang out with him, things had to be kept on a superficial level—every time he tried to have a meaningful conversation with her, she pretty much kicked him to the curb. Which was a lot more annoying than he had expected it to be, especially this week, as he was preparing to head overseas for a few weeks.

Since Reece had gotten married, Matt had been doing most of the traveling, which was normally fine with him. But now, with Camille and a baby on the way, he found himself wanting to stick closer to home.

He'd tried to talk to Camille about it the night before, but she'd blown him off. Tonight he wouldn't let her, he decided as he let himself into the house.

He went to set his keys in the bowl he kept on the entryway table for just that purpose and found it filled with orange-scented potpourri—and the table it rested on was cluttered with mail, magazines and a bunch of other indecipherable junk.

Ignoring the mess, he headed through the great room to the kitchen. On his way, he did his best to ignore the fact that his beloved poker table was loaded down with bags from the closest art supply store.

Bottles of paint, brushes and other art supplies tumbled haphazardly out of the bags, and he gritted his teeth when he saw the smears of red pigment that crisscrossed the green felt. Trying to keep his cool, he averted his eyes, but it was difficult. A man's poker table should be sacrosanct, certainly above being used as a rest stop for a bunch of painting stuff.

He stepped into the kitchen and realized Hurricane Camille had struck in here, as well. A cereal bowl and some glasses were in the sink and a frying pan was on the stove, a grilled cheese sandwich still resting in it—as if she had made it, then forgotten to eat it. The crumpled cheese wrappers and half-used butter container were still on the counter.

Shaking his head, he reached into the fridge to grab a beer and came away with a tall can of paint thinner instead. *Paint thinner?* He stared at the container for long seconds, then burst into laughter. How could he not? Camille certainly knew how to keep a man on his toes.

When she'd first moved in, he'd been more than a little concerned about the chaos that seemed to follow wherever she led. But lately, he'd learned to appreciate her particular brand of absentminded mess. Which was more than a little disconcerting, now that he thought about it. How far gone was a guy when he found endearing things that would normally irritate the hell out of him?

Because he didn't want to dwell on his feelings for Camille—and the confusion that came with those feelings—he dropped the paint thinner on the counter and made sure that when he reached into the fridge this time he came out with a bottle of beer.

Popping the top on it, he headed back toward the family room and his TV, but on the way, he noticed that the answering machine light was blinking—despite the fact that Camille's electric-yellow Volkswagen was in the driveway. She'd bought the secondhand car a few days ago.

He absently hit the play button, then picked up the remote control and started flipping through the channels, looking for the game. He only half listened as his mother extolled the virtues of her daughters—all of whom remembered to call her daily—and completely ignored a message from a carpet-cleaning service. But when the third message came on, he sprung to full alertness, the Texas Rangers game completely forgotten.

Camille, this is Dr. D'Amato's office. The doctor wanted me to call and remind you that time was running out on the blood test you discussed at your last appointment. To be effective, it has to be done no later than next Friday. Please call us at 555-2761 to set up an appointment.

Blood test? Matt stared at the answering machine in confusion. He'd missed Camille's last checkup because of a meeting at work, but they'd talked about it when he'd gotten home. She'd never mentioned anything about a blood test.

Probably because she'd figured he'd drag her across town to get it done right away—and she would have been correct. He could put up with the mess and the chaos and the fact that she was always fifteen minutes late, but he just couldn't understand her penchant for procrastination—especially when it came to their baby.

Why hadn't she arranged to have the test done? he wondered again, as he headed toward her studio to ask her. She was probably knee-deep in the painting she'd started a few days before and would throw a fit about being disturbed, but at that moment he didn't much care. The child she carried was his, and he had a right to be kept informed of what was going on. If she was ducking a blood test, he wanted to know why.

She'd probably have some excuse about how she was too busy with the commissions she'd gotten since moving back to Austin to fit in a run to the doctor's. But he wasn't taking any chances with her health—or the baby's. He'd call first thing in the morning and get an appointment—and he'd go with her to make sure that it got done.

Her studio door was closed, which was unusual enough that it gave him pause. Still, trying to be polite, he knocked once. Twice. But by the third time, when she hadn't answered, he began imagining her passed out on the floor, injured or miscarrying.

It was an illogical leap, but one he couldn't help making even as he told himself he was being ridiculous. Camille was probably engrossed in her art—the world could go by while she was painting and she wouldn't notice.

He knocked again, to no avail. To hell with it—he was going in. Pushing the door open, he scanned his old loft. Camille had made a bunch of superficial changes, but he barely registered them as he glanced around, frantic to find her.

His entire body stiffened, then relaxed, when he caught sight of her curled up on the couch, her knees drawn toward her chest in an unconscious fetal position.

He walked across the room, stood over her. Checked to make sure her chest was rising and falling even as he told himself he was an idiot. It was. He told himself to leave, told himself that she was fine and he was invading her privacy by watching her sleep.

But he didn't move, except to crouch down next to her. It had been months since he'd seen her sleep, months since he'd sat up at night watching the play of emotions across her face. She was more beautiful—and more heartbreaking—than he remembered.

She was also exhausted. Though her first trimester had come and gone, she was still tired all the time. More than once she had almost fallen asleep at the dinner table. He'd called Rick and asked about it a few weeks ago, as all the books said she should be feeling energetic in her second trimester. The doctor had laughed at him and told him to stop worrying. All women were different, and for a woman as slender as Camille, carrying a baby was difficult work.

He'd doubled his campaign to get her to eat more and she'd obliged him, but it didn't seem like any of the food was sticking. She was as thin as ever, except for the small bump that had begun pressing against the front of her T-shirts.

He'd also suggested that she slow down, not take on as many paintings and temp jobs, but she'd merely laughed at him. She needed the money, she'd said, and after years of having to make her living doing office temp jobs, she was thrilled to finally have enough portrait business to build up her savings.

The first part of her answer had infuriated him, as he had more than enough money to support all three of them. But he hadn't argued—not then, and not at the beginning of the month when she'd written him a rent check to cover her bedroom and studio.

No matter how much he hated it, he'd kept his mouth shut and taken her money. She'd be in the wind if he didn't. The fact that he was putting her rent money into the college fund he'd started for the baby soon after he'd learned Camille was pregnant was small comfort.

As he watched her sleep, she squirmed around, as if looking for a comfortable spot. For most people, sleep was a peaceful time, but for Camille—with her boundless energy and unmentionable past—it was simply a drop into the unconscious, a time when all of the feelings she kept hidden during the day were released.

Just like now. Her brow was wrinkled, her lips pursed, her shoulders hunched—she looked as if she were in pain, or about to ward off a painful blow. Her arms circled her growing belly protectively and her back bowed outward.

It hurt to see her like this, more than it had months ago when he'd begged her to stay. As he'd watched her the past few weeks, listened to what she said—and more important, to what she didn't—he'd come to realize that Camille had demons, demons she didn't trust him enough to mention. He couldn't help wondering if those demons were the cause of her exhaustion.

Reaching a hand out, he stroked it softly over her wild gypsy curls. She smelled like strawberries and cream and warm, sweet woman. He breathed deeply, took the scent inside of himself even as he tangled his fingers in her miles of hair.

It felt so good to be close to her, even like this. So good to touch her, when it had been weeks since she'd let him do more than awkwardly shake her hand.

Weeks since he'd kissed her as if she was his entire world.

Weeks since he'd admitted his fears to Rhiannon—and himself.

Though he was still determined to protect himself from her, determined not to fall for her again just to watch her walk away, he didn't move from her side.

He couldn't—he was spellbound by the soft sounds she made in her sleep and the miles of skin exposed by her cherry-red tank top and black maternity shorts.

He longed to touch her, and a drop of sweat rolled down his back as he resisted the urge. Stroking her hair while she slept was one thing, but copping a feel was another thing entirely. Even without touching all of her creamy skin, his body was reacting. Hardening to the point of pain. Reminding him just how long it had been since he'd been with a woman.

There'd been nobody since his last time with Camille, and that had been about five months before. But he didn't want anyone else—he was smart enough to know that only Camille would do.

Because the thought sent ice skating up his spine, he pulled away abruptly. Reached for the afghan draped across the back of the couch and covered Camille with it. He still wanted to talk to her about the doctor's appointment, but it could wait. Better to let her sleep—she needed it. And he needed time to remind himself of all the reasons trusting Camille was a bad idea.

Letting himself out of her studio, he went in search of food—doing something concrete would keep his mind off the intangible struggle of emotions inside him. And if it didn't, at least it would keep his hands—and mouth—busy.

CAMILLE PLOWED INTO consciousness the way some women worked their way through a shoe sale at Nordstrom's—with power, deliberation and a great deal of steely determination.

It had always been like that for her. One brief moment of vulnerability followed by a calculated crash into armored reality. Lazing around in that hazy state between sleep and wakefulness wasn't for her—it was dangerous there, filled with unguarded thoughts and undeniable emotions. When she was young, it was the time when the monsters had come—when she'd been hurt or afraid and there'd been no one turn to.

These days she made sure she relied on herself, that she was never vulnerable enough to need someone to comfort her.

Sitting up, she glanced around the shadowed room, tried to get her bearings. Was she in Italy? Paris? New York? Her gaze fell on the long picture window that ran the length of the room and she abruptly remembered. She was in Austin. At Matt's house. Pregnant.

How deeply had she been sleeping that she could have forgotten any of that, even for a moment? It wasn't as if thoughts of the baby—and Matt—didn't rule her every waking hour.

Because thinking of Matt when she was still warm from sleep made her feel vulnerable—and even a little aroused—she quickly climbed to her feet, then went into the attached bathroom and splashed cold water on her face. It was dark outside and Matt should be home any minute—she should get dinner ready.

She went back into her studio and searched for the slippers she always wore, because Matt's wood floors hurt her feet after a while. She found them behind a prepped canvas, but when she bent to pick them up, she lost her balance and nearly fell flat on her face.

In an effort to save herself, she threw a hand out to grab on to something—and ended up putting her fist right through the canvas she'd prepped a few hours before.

She stared at the mess and couldn't help wondering what was happening to her. The book Matt had gotten her said pregnant woman had a tendency to be unsteady as their stomachs grew—something about not being used to the new weight distribution. She'd thought it odd when she read it, but obviously there was something to the theory.

Yet one more thing to look forward to with this pregnancy, as if incessant exhaustion, skin breakouts and swollen ankles weren't already more fun than she could handle.

Hot, annoyed and thoroughly put out with the entire world, she made her way slowly down the stairs, making sure to hang on to the banister as she did. With her luck, she'd averted a fall in the studio just to tumble down the steps.

She was about halfway down the stairs when she heard the unmistakable sound of a ballgame—and a knife repeatedly striking a cutting board. She'd slept through his arrival. A shiver of unease moved through her as she wondered if he'd come looking for her, if he'd watched her while she slept. She had a tendency to have nightmares, and to talk in her sleep, which was why she rarely took lovers. It was even rarer for her to stay with one afterward. In fact, Matt was the only man she could ever remember sleeping with—why hadn't she realized that before? And how stupid was she to repeatedly make herself vulnerable to a man who found it so easy to push her away?

More freaked out by the revelation than she wanted to admit, Camille gingerly made her way through the family room to the kitchen. On the way, she realized for the first time how messy she'd let Matt's house get. After dinner, she'd have to straighten things up—no matter how comfortable she felt here, she needed to remember that this arrangement was just temporary. This was Matt's home and she didn't belong here, not on any permanent basis, anyway.

"Hey. I thought I heard you in here. Did you get a good nap?"

She straightened so quickly that she hit her head on the floor lamp she was standing under. For a second she saw stars, and her hands clutched her head defensively.

Matt swore as he crossed the room. "Are you okay? I didn't mean to startle you." Gentle hands cupped her face as his long, graceful fingers probed her scalp.

"I'm fine." Was that her sounding so breathless? She clenched her teeth against the knee-jerk reaction, told herself to get a grip.

"I heard the crack all the way across the room. You'll probably have— Yep, here's the bump."

"Ouch!" She sucked in her breath as he poked at the tender spot.

"Sorry. Let's get you some ice." He turned toward the kitchen, his hand on her lower back to guide her.

"I'm fine, Matt. I don't need ice."

"You do if you don't want to have a permanent bump there. They calcify quickly, you know."

"Since I have no plans to go bald anytime soon, I don't really consider that a problem."

"Still." He tugged her along as he always did, pushing and prodding at her until she found herself seated at the kitchen table, holding a bag of ice over her injury. She couldn't believe how much it rankled.

"How do you do that?" she asked as Matt returned to the cutting board.

"Chop peppers?" He tossed a surprised look over his shoulder.

"Get me to do whatever you want."

"I don't."

"Sure you do." She gestured with the ice. "I'm sitting here with an ice pack I don't want, getting a headache from the cold against my little bump."

"First of all, it's not a little bump. Second of all, it only makes sense that you treat yourself when you're injured. Surely that has nothing to do with me."

"I don't know about that."

"Camille." Matt regarded her with amusement, even as he set the vegetables to sauté in the pan. "You make me sound like some kind of bully."

"Not a bully. Just determined to get your own way. Always convinced that you're right."

"In this case, I *am* right."

"That's not the point!" she huffed in frustration.

"Then what is the point?" He turned the element temperature to low, then crossed the room and crouched down next to her, so that they were eye to eye. "What's wrong, Camille?"

His eyes were filled with compassion and she felt her own well with unexpected—but now familiar—tears. She dashed a hand across her eyes, hoped he wouldn't notice. "I don't like being handled."

He reared back. "Is that what you think I'm doing? Handling you?"

"Yes. No. I don't know." He was crowding her, pushing her, his big body so close she could feel the heat radiating from him. A part of her found the warmth comforting, but at the same time she felt stifled. Overwhelmed.

"What do you mean you don't know? Either you feel handled, or you don't."

She couldn't breathe, panic welling up inside of her for no reason that she could really understand. Shoving at Matt's shoulders, she tried to scoot her chair back, to put some distance between them. To get away.

Matt took the hint and stood up abruptly, crossing back to the stove without another word. His back was straight, his shoulders tense, and she hadn't missed the flash of hurt in his eyes before he turned away from her.

"Look, Matt, I'm sorry." She really didn't feel like apologizing, but figured she owed it to him since she'd been the one to pick at him, when all he'd been trying to do was help.

"Don't be." He dropped more vegetables in the pan, lifted the chicken breasts onto a plate to rest.

"Matt—"

"Drop it, Camille."

"So that's it?" she asked, her annoyance rekindling instantaneously. "You don't want to talk about it so we don't? And you wonder why I feel handled?"

The fork he was holding hit the granite countertop with a crash. "You want to talk, Camille. Fine, let's talk. There was a message from Rick's office on the machine—you need to go in for a blood test but you keep dodging it. What blood test is it and why didn't you tell me about it?"

"Because it's nothing—it's unimportant."

"Obviously Rick doesn't think so, or he wouldn't have his staff calling to make an appointment. So what test are we talking about here?"

"It's an optional test—for Down's syndrome." She winced as Matt turned pale. "See? That's why I didn't tell you. I knew you'd freak out."

"Rick thinks the baby has Down's syndrome?"

"No. Of course not. But they offer a test for it. It's completely optional, but Rick suggested I have it because I'm over thirty and that increases the risk a little bit."

"Let me get this straight." Matt spoke through gritted teeth. "There's a chance our baby could have Down's syndrome. Rick wants to test for it because you're over thirty, and you're procrastinating?" The last was said at almost a yell—something Matt rarely did and which told her just how upset he was.

"There's a one-in-five-hundred chance that *any* baby will have Down's syndrome. And I'm not procrastinating. I have no intention of getting that test."

MATT STARED AT CAMILLE in disbelief as her words echoed through the kitchen. "Of course you're going to have the test."

"No, I'm not."

There was a roaring in his ears, and his stomach was one big knot as he tried to come to grips with her matter-of-fact words. "Camille, this is our baby we're talking about. If there's a chance he or she has a problem, we need to know about it."

"Why?"

"What do you mean why? Are you being deliberately dense?"

"No. I'm serious. Why do we need to know? Is it going to change anything?"

"It can change everything. It—"

"Really?" She cocked her head to the side. "What exactly is it going to change, Matt? Am I going to have an abortion?"

"Of course not!" He thrust a hand through his hair, feeling as if his entire world was crumbling around him. "Jesus. I can't believe you'd even suggest that."

"I'm not suggesting it. I'm telling you why I don't want to have the stupid test. We're in agreement that I'm not going to have an abortion, so what's the point? If the baby does have Down's syndrome, there's nothing they can do until he or she is born anyway."

She walked toward him, holding her hand out imploringly, but he could barely hear her over the shock ripping through him. "I did my research, Matt, I swear I did. And there's a high chance of a false positive, which will lead to more invasive tests that may or may not be able to tell for sure. Not to mention the fact that it will completely freak us out for the remainder of the pregnancy."

"Camille, this is our child's well-being we're talking about." How could she not see that? How could she not understand that they needed to take every precaution? Knowledge was power. How could he plan for the unexpected if he didn't know whether or not the baby was sick?

"Not taking the test won't hurt our child in the least."

"You don't know that."

"Sure, I do. If there is something wrong with the baby, we can't fix it. And if we get a positive result from the test, it means Rick will have to do an amniocentesis, which—besides hurting like hell—carries with it all kinds of risks to the baby, including infection and miscarriage."

"But if something's wrong—" He knew he sounded like a broken record, but he couldn't help it. He'd been blindsided by this, stunned by her inability to see his side of the story.

"If something's wrong, we'll deal with it—*after* the baby is born."

"So that's it? I don't even get a vote?"

"Of course you get a vote. I—"

"There's no 'of course' about it. You weren't even going to tell me about the test. If I hadn't heard that message, I would never even have known it was an option. Isn't that right?"

She shifted uncomfortably and he felt the shock melting, being replaced by anger. "I thought we were partners, Camille. I thought we were in this together."

"We are."

"Bullshit. You were going to make this decision on your own. Actually, you're still making it on your own. What I want—what I think about it—doesn't matter to you at all."

"Now you're being ridiculous."

"I'm ridiculous? You're the one who won't even consider my point of view."

"I've considered your viewpoint. I have," she insisted when he looked at her with patent disbelief. "But I don't agree with it."

"So that's it. We're back to the fact that I don't get a say in my baby's welfare—at least not while it's in your body."

"Of course you do. Why are you being so stubborn about this?"

"Why are you being so absurd about it? You're burying your head in the sand like a damn ostrich—if you can't see the threat, it doesn't exist."

"I can't talk to you when you're like this. When you're ready to be reasonable, come find me." She spun around, headed for the door, but he was two steps ahead of her. His palm hit the doorway with a thud, effectively blocking her exit.

"Get out of my way, Matt." It was her turn to speak through clenched teeth, but he was too far gone to care.

"Not until we finish talking about this."

"We are finished talking about this."

"Because you say so?"

"Because you're acting like a Neanderthal." She shoved at his arm. "I won't put up with you trying to frighten me into seeing things your way."

His eyes narrowed and he leaned forward until mere inches separated them. "Is that what you think I'm doing? Trying to scare you?"

"What would you call it?" she challenged.

"Going out of my freaking mind! I know we're not the best of friends or anything, but shit, don't you know me at all, Camille?"

"What's that supposed to mean?"

"I've never used force to intimidate a woman in my life and I really don't appreciate being accused of it by you."

"Well, then, don't tower over me like some crazy man bent on getting his own way."

"You're the one determined to get her own way."

"That's a joke." She took a deep breath, seemed to be considering her next words carefully. When she finally spoke, it was like a knife in the gut. "I'm not some doll you can bend this way or that to suit your moods or beliefs, Matt. I'm a person and sometimes I want to do things my way. Even if it's different from yours. It doesn't make it wrong."

"When have I ever said your way was wrong?"

"How about right now?"

"This time you *are* wrong."

"Why? Because I don't agree with you?"

"Because you don't agree with the doctor! If Rick wants you to take the test—"

"Rick wants every pregnant woman to take that stupid test! That doesn't mean it's necessary."

"It doesn't mean it isn't, either."

"Back off, Matt."

"Or what? You'll run away?" The words slipped out before he could stop them, but once they were said he couldn't regret them. He'd lived with the cloud of her taking off for weeks now and it was wearing on him, big-time, just like Rhiannon had predicted.

Camille let out a strangled scream. "There you go again, with the same old argument. But I'm not the one holding this relationship hostage. You are. You're the one who's always making plans without me, then leaving me to catch up. Whether it was picking out my obstetrician or deciding what we have for dinner or convincing me to move in with you. Everything we do is always *your* way."

He stared at her, speechless, for nearly a full minute, and when he finally did speak, he concentrated on keeping his voice low, controlled. Otherwise he just might start screaming and never stop. "Yes, Camille, it's all my way. Having you move into my house and turn it into a pigpen is definitely what I wanted. Not getting a vote in whether or not you take an important blood test that concerns my child is certainly my first choice. Dealing with your mood swings and your suspicions, worrying about when you're going to run off and to where and if I'll ever get the chance to see my baby, yes, that's all my way."

He literally vibrated with anger. "You have all the power, Camille, and we both know it. So don't pretend that you're the injured party here, that you're just being pushed along by big, bad me. Because it doesn't play and frankly, it's beneath you."

He slammed out of the kitchen, leaving her staring after him while his carefully chopped vegetables smoldered on the stove.

CHAPTER TEN

MATT WALKED THE STREETS furiously, his mind replaying his fight with Camille with every step he took. What the hell was wrong with her? How could she accuse him of intimidation, when he'd bent over backward to make things easy for her? When he'd switched his whole life around to accommodate her and a baby he hadn't planned for? What more could he do for her, short of severing one of his damn limbs?

What exactly had she done for him lately—except wreak havoc on his life and his libido? Sure, he'd been the one to suggest that they not renew their romantic relationship, but he'd only been doing what he thought was right. And she sure as hell had punished him for that, hadn't she? Waltzing around in her little tank tops and short-shorts, her newly rounded curves distracting him with every move she made.

And she had the nerve to call him manipulative? She was the one who had made an important decision regarding their child without so much as consulting him.

He kept up his angry pace, tackling block after block in the stifling July heat, aware of nothing but his own thoughts and the sweat rolling damply down his back. Camille was a piece of work, that was for sure. He'd given her everything he could and still it wasn't good enough. Worse, she had the nerve to say it wasn't what she'd wanted. That she'd wanted something else entirely, but had never bothered to clue him in before.

He made a right turn onto Willow Lane, heading toward Reece's house with the intention of having a good, old-fashioned bitch fest. After all, if a man couldn't complain to his best friend, whom could he complain to? But when he stopped in front of Reece's house, it was to find his friend playing baseball in the yard with his seven-year-old twins, Justin and Johnny.

"Hey, buddy, what are you doing over here?" Reece called, jogging down the driveway.

Matt ground his teeth together, forced himself to be polite when the last thing he wanted to do was see Reece blissfully ensconced with his happy, happy family. How was he supposed to complain when the kids were underfoot?

"Just out for a walk."

Reece eyed him knowingly. "You look like a man on a mission—or one with woman troubles. Come on in and have a drink."

Matt shook his head. "Are you sure?" He gestured to the boys. "You look kind of busy."

"Nah, it's fine. We were just about to go in anyway. It's sundae night—come on in and have some sugar. I'll run you home afterward."

"Yeah, Uncle Matt! Stay! Pleeease!" Johnny looked at him expectantly. "Mom always dishes out more ice cream if we have company."

Matt laughed despite his bad mood. "Nice to know I'm good for something." But he started climbing the stairs that led to the front door.

"Perfect timing, guys." Reece's wife, Sarah, called from the kitchen. "I've got everything on the table."

"We've got an extra guest, honey." Reece led them all into the kitchen, where he dropped a lingering kiss on Sarah's lips before turning to blow raspberries on his eighteen-month-old daughter's tummy. Rose chortled in delight.

"Matt! It's good to see you." Sarah's smile lit up the room. She looked so healthy and well-rested that it was hard to imagine she'd given birth a few short weeks before. Maybe he should tap Reece for their secrets—especially since he and Camille were ready to tear each other's hair out and the baby hadn't even arrived yet.

"Hey, where's the baby?" Matt asked, glancing around the crowded kitchen.

"In his bassinet in the family room." Sarah nodded toward the doorway. "You can go take a look if you want."

"I do." Tiptoeing into the darkened family room, he peered into the bassinet at little Jacob Anthony. A sense of wonder filled him as he looked at the baby's little fingers, at his small head and delicate features. He was so small, yet already Matt could see how he'd grown in the weeks since he'd stood with Reece, checking him out through the window of the hospital nursery.

It seemed impossible that in a few short months he would have one of these tiny creatures. A baby that depended completely on Camille and him. The idea warmed him, until his doubts crept in. Would he ever get the chance to do the things with his child that Reece took for granted? Or would he be relegated to the role of part-time father, only seeing the baby when Camille was in town—or when he traveled to wherever she was?

It was a sobering thought, and one that he was sure would haunt him in the months to come.

He didn't know how long he stood there, looking down at the little guy, thinking about what it would be like to be responsible for something so slight, so utterly dependent.

"He's pretty cool, huh?" Reece came up on the other side of the bassinet and peered into it, as if he, too, couldn't believe that he'd helped create such a tiny, perfect human being.

"I'll say. You and Sarah make beautiful babies."

"We try." His friend's grin split his face from ear to ear. "But come on, let's get some ice cream. There's a rumor going around that Sarah picked up some Chunky Monkey."

"Well, by all means, I don't want to be left out of that."

"That's what I figured."

Matt spent the next few minutes loading up on ice cream and laughing at the twins' antics as they tried to outdo each other in a contest to see who could get the most ice cream in his mouth in one bite. Reece put an end to the competition with a monster bite of chocolate ice cream loaded with sprinkles and whipped cream.

"Ugh, Dad, that's disgusting!" Justin crowed in delight.

"Disgusting!" Johnny echoed. "Do it again!"

"I think once is enough for this lifetime," Sarah interjected drily. "Now, everyone finish up—at a normal rate—please. It's bath time in T minus five minutes."

"Cool! Bath time. Can we try out the new submarine, Mom?"

"That was supposed to be for the swimming pool," Sarah replied over her shoulder as she wiped down the counters.

"Aww, come on! If you let us take a bath in your tub it'll be plenty big enough!"

"You're supposed to take a bath in your bathroom," his mother said.

"Just for tonight! Pleeease!" Johnny stuck out his trembling lower lip in the most pathetic pout Matt had ever seen, but Sarah merely laughed.

"All right, guys. Tonight only."

"Yay!"

"All right!"

"I get first dibs!" Johnny called as he raced his brother for the stairs.

"No way! You got to pick the color—that means I get to play with it first."

"Yeah, but I picked yellow because it's your favorite color. That means I should get it first."

Sarah rolled her eyes as she poked her husband in the stomach. "I blame you for this."

"For what?" Reece asked with mock innocence.

"For getting them the submarine in the first place. Whoever heard of a remote control sub in the bathtub, for God's sake?"

"That's what you get for picking out such a big tub," he said.

"You've never complained before," she shot back as she started up the stairs after her sons. "I'll be ready for Rosie in about twenty minutes—will you bring her up then?"

"You bet."

"And keep an eye on Jake?"

"Well, I was considering feeding him to the neighborhood dogs, but if you insist...."

"Aren't you the comedian?"

Reece watched his wife climb the stairs, then turned to Matt with a grin. "So, what's Camille done to get you so up in arms?"

"I'm not 'up in arms'!" Matt answered, offended by the description. "I just needed a little break."

"Aww, come on." For a minute Reece sounded just like one of the twins. "This is me, buddy. I know you better than just about anybody."

"And?"

"And you've got your boxers twisted up so tightly it's amazing you can still walk." He paused. "So come on, spill. Did she leave her shoes out? Drop paint on the carpet? Forget to do the dishes?"

"You make it sound like I'm totally OCD."

"Not OCD. Just...particular."

"I'm not that bad."

"So she didn't do any of that stuff? Nothing? I think I'm disappointed. I expected better from your girl."

"She's not my girl. And yes, she did all of that stuff—except the paint on the carpet. She got it on the poker table instead."

"Wow. And she's still alive?"

"Shut up."

Reece laughed. "You've got to loosen up a little, buddy. Once the baby comes, nothing will be sacred. You've seen Justin and Johnny in action enough to know that."

Matt sighed, gave up the fight. "That wasn't even what set me off. I mean, sure, it pissed me off that she's basically turned my house into chaos central, but I'm dealing with that."

"Are you?"

"Yes! I am," he insisted when Reece looked skeptical. "But then she comes in the kitchen and picks a fight with me for no reason at all and somehow I'm the bad guy in all this."

"Get used to that, man. Pregnancy hormones are killers."

"How would you know? Sarah's the sweetest woman on the planet."

"That's because you haven't seen her seven months pregnant and jonesing for chocolate. It isn't pretty."

"Give me a break."

"I'm serious, man. She becomes a fire-breathing dragon. Ask the boys—for a while it was every man for himself around here."

"Yeah, she looks real dangerous."

"Neither does Camille. But here you are."

"Yeah, but that's different. She's driving me crazy. And then she decides she's not going to take this blood test that Rick thinks she should have. I tried to talk to her, to voice my opinion on the subject, and she completely shot me down. Like I shouldn't even get a vote. Then suddenly we're fighting not just about the test, but about everything."

He paused for a minute and then blurted out what had sent him over the edge. "I'm doing my best to be helpful and supportive, trying to do the right thing, and she accuses me of trying to run her life, saying that I just barged in and took over like some kind of tank on a mission."

"Aah."

"What does that mean? Aah, what?"

Reece cleared his throat. "You *can* be kind of controlling. In the best way, of course, but still—"

"Controlling?" Matt was beginning to feel like a damn parrot, but he couldn't help himself. "I don't try to control her."

"No, of course not."

"So I found her an obstetrician? Why shouldn't I, when Rick's right here in town? It's not like she has medical insurance and she won't let me pay for anything, so what's wrong with taking her to a friend who won't charge her for the visits? Especially when he's a damn good doctor?"

"Nothing."

"Exactly. And she didn't have to move in with me if she didn't want to. It was just the most expedient solution for the time being."

"Of course it was."

"And so what if I make sure there's a bunch of fruits and vegetables in the house? All the baby books stress how important nutrition is and it's not like Camille can live on ice cream alone, no matter how much she might want to."

"You're absolutely right," Reece choked out.

"And God forbid I try to pay for something every once in a while. You'd think a movie ticket was a frickin' diamond ring the way she—" He broke off as a suspicious sound came from his best friend. "You're laughing at me!"

"I'm not."

"Really?" He raised an eyebrow. "What would you call it? Rhythmic convulsions?"

Reece gave up the ghost and busted out with a huge bellow of laughter, one that went on so long that Matt could actually feel his back teeth grinding together.

"Are you finished?"

"Almost?" Reece howled, wiping his eyes with the back of his hand.

"You know what, I don't need this shit. *You're* the one who invited *me* in."

"And you're the one who showed up at my doorstep at eight o'clock at night. You think that's a coincidence?"

Matt didn't bother trying to pretend that he hadn't set out for Reece's deliberately. His friend knew him well enough to know when he was lying. "So, you want to give me that ride home now?"

"Sure. Just let me run Rosie upstairs." He snagged his keys off the counter, tossed them to Matt. "I'll meet you in the garage."

They spent the ride home talking about guy stuff— baseball, cars, the new building set to begin construction in Tokyo—for which Matt was grateful. He really didn't need any more touchy-feely crap, especially if all it did was give Reece a great laugh at his expense.

But when they were almost to his house, Reece glanced over at him and said, "You know, things are going to work out. You just need to give it a little time."

"I know that."

"Do you? Because I figure you're freaking out about the little stuff—and so is she, by the way, because neither of you know what the future holds."

"It holds a baby, Reece. I'm not an idiot."

"I'm not talking about the baby. I think that's probably the least confusing part of this whole mess."

"I don't know what you mean." Matt stared straight out the window, even as he focused completely on what Reece was saying.

"Yes, you do. Adjusting to a new baby, especially an unexpected one, is difficult, sure. But not overly complicated. Your problem is you still have feelings for Camille."

"That's absurd."

"Don't forget who you're talking to here. I've known you since you were a pimply faced eighteen-year-old kid away from home for the first time."

"I could say the same thing about you."

"Yes, you could. Which is why I know how conflicted you are about Camille. I saw you last winter— you were crazy about her, in a way you've never been about a woman in the eighteen years I've known you. That kind of loss of control wouldn't have sat easy with you in the best of circumstances. Add in the fact that she walked out on you? How can it be anything *but* complicated?"

"I'm not the one complicating things. She is. It all started because I wanted her to take a simple blood test—"

"You want my advice? Don't fight her on it."

Matt did turn to stare at him then, completely flummoxed. "How can you say that? What if the baby has Down's syndrome?"

"What if it does? What if it doesn't? Is knowing going to change anything?"

"That's what Camille said."

"She's a smart woman—maybe you should start listening to her for a change."

As Matt climbed out of the car, he couldn't help wondering if Reece was right. But how could he listen to Camille when she so rarely confided in him?

CAMILLE PACED THE FAMILY ROOM for what had to be the twentieth time since Matt had walked out, cursing herself from one wall to the other.

So what if he was mad? So what if he hadn't liked what she'd had to say? So what if he ended up asking her to leave? It wasn't the first time she'd been on her own and it wouldn't be the last. She was a big girl and it was ridiculous that she was sitting here, wringing her hands and worrying about the fact that she'd had a fight with Matt.

He wasn't her husband, wasn't her boyfriend. Wasn't anything but the father of her baby, and she'd do well to remember that. Besides, since when was she the kind of woman to sit around waiting for a man to come back?

Since she'd been the one to hurt him for no reason.

As she finally acknowledged the truth, Camille tripped over her favorite pair of Birkenstock sandals for what had to be the tenth time. With a muffled oath, she picked them up, then crossed to the entry hall, deposited them in the front coat closet and did her damnedest to convince herself that the reason she was staring out the front window had absolutely nothing to do with Matt.

It turned out she was no better at lying to herself than she was at keeping house. She glanced around the entryway as the things Matt had said during the fight continued to circle in her brain. The house *was* a mess and she *was* responsible for it. Yet Matt, who had a place for everything, hadn't said a word to her about it until she'd basically told him his opinion didn't matter to her.

He was right. She did have a nerve. Oh, he hadn't said those exact words, but he'd implied the hell out of them in his parting shot.

She hadn't deliberately set out to keep the blood test from him. But she knew herself, knew she couldn't survive the rest of the pregnancy knowing there was something wrong with her child and that she couldn't do anything about it. And Matt was such a control freak, she figured he'd go insane if the test came back positive—even false positive. It had seemed better all the way around to just wait and let things play out the way they were supposed to.

Maybe she'd been wrong. No, she sighed as she scooped up the piles of paper and mail from the entry-way table and carried them into the kitchen, where she sorted through them, tossing everything she didn't want and stacking anything Matt might need in one neat pile. There was no "maybe" about it. She had been wrong. Maybe if she'd told him her point of view instead of getting her back up, they could have talked about things like rational adults instead of having a pissing contest that had gotten them absolutely nowhere.

After she finished with the mail, she moved into the family room and did the same thing with her art supplies, carrying them up to her studio.

She had a bad moment or ten when she realized her tube of red paint had leaked on his poker table, then remembered that she was using water-based paints because the fumes from the oil were bad for the baby. A few hard scrubs and the table was back to normal—as long as she didn't look too closely. She was hoping the residual stain would fade out as the felt dried.

Why had she been so cruel to Matt at the end? she wondered furiously as she swept through the rest of the house, cleaning up various and sundry messes as she went. Because he'd cared enough about her and the baby to worry about what was best for them?

Sure, she was dead-on when she said he was a bit overbearing and a little too domineering, but effort had to count for something. He'd never complained about the baby, never demanded that she get an abortion. He'd just buckled down and gotten straight to work, making her life as easy as possible.

Maybe that's what was bothering her, Camille acknowledged as she finished cleaning up the dishes in the sink. Matt had everything together—he had a job he loved, a family he adored, good friends, a nice house. He had the whole enchilada, and what did she have, except for a few canvasses, a bunch of paint-stained clothes and a stomach that seemed to be growing bigger every second?

Not for the first time she wished she had someone to talk to. But her way of life didn't exactly lend itself to long, deep friendships. The few friends she had were more like acquaintances. Party pals.

And unlike Matt, she didn't have a big family to turn to. For fifteen years it had been just her and she'd always liked it that way—no responsibilities, no ties. But now, as she sat here racking her brain about Matt and their future, it sure would be nice to have someone to talk to.

How sick was it that the only person in her life she could really count on was the same one who was currently giving her fits?

It's not that she begrudged Matt what he had—he deserved all the good fortune in the world. But at the same time, she wished she had more. More friends, a better family, a job that paid more than recycling cans.

For the first time in her life, she wasn't happy with who she was and the life she led. How was she supposed to measure up to Matt? How was she supposed to meet him on even ground, when he had so much going for him and she had so little? It was like looking at her parents' marriage, her mother trapped and at her father's mercy because he was the one with all the power, all the support.

She'd always sworn that she would never let that happen to her, that she would never get seriously involved with a man who had all the power in the relationship. And she could protest all she wanted, tell herself that she didn't seriously care about Matt, but it would be a lie. He was the father of her child and the only man in a very long time who could make her heart beat faster with just a look, who could curl her toes with a quick skim of his lips against hers.

She wasn't planning for a big happily ever after—didn't want one if it meant she had to give up her freedom. But it would be nice to feel as though she was on even footing, as though she stood a chance next to Matt and his star-kissed life.

She heard a car pass by and resisted the urge to run to the front door and check for Matt, yet again. Besides,

he was on foot. But he should be back any second now—
he'd been gone for nearly two hours. How far could the
man walk—

The sound of a key turning in the front door lock had
her springing to her feet like a puppet on a string.

CHAPTER ELEVEN

MATT LET THE DOOR CLOSE behind him, went to toss his keys in the bowl on the table, then stopped himself at the last minute. Orange-scented potpourri. Right. Taking over his house and his life, one key bowl at a time.

But the table was cleared off, the mail sorted into one neat pile the way he liked it, so he dropped his keys on the table and headed farther into the house. The rooms were dark, the only light coming from the small lamp above the stove.

He wondered where Camille was, whether she'd gone to sleep already or if she was painting. Wondered briefly if she'd left, then discounted the idea. Reece had dropped him next to her Volkswagen.

"Matt."

He turned toward the family room and Camille's husky tone. "Camille."

"I'm sorry." The words were stiff, disjointed, and he strained to see her face in the heavy shadows.

"What for?"

"What—" She paused, took a deep breath. "Right. I have a lot to apologize for. I'm sorry for picking that stupid fight. For the things I said. For—"

"That's not what I meant." He crossed to her, flipping a side lamp on as he walked. "You were right. I can be difficult and overbearing. Convinced that I'm right, that my way is the only—"

"No, you were just trying to have a say in what happens to the baby—which is your right. If the test means that much to you I'll call Rick in the morning and schedule a time to go in. I am—"

He cut her off with a finger on her lips. They were as soft as he remembered and that spark kindled deep inside him, the one that had gotten them into this situation to begin with.

"Is this really necessary? Us tripping over apologies when we can just move on? Do what you think is best in this situation. I'll support you whether you take the test or not."

Something flickered in her eyes, something that was there and gone so fast that he could barely register it, other than to know that it made him nervous. Very, very nervous.

But when she spoke, her voice was normal. "I appreciate your support." She stepped back. "Did you eat?"

"I had an ice cream sundae with my friend Reece and his kids. How about you?"

"No. I...wasn't hungry. Plus, I was waiting for you."

"Well, let's go see what we've got." He headed into the kitchen, then stopped himself. "If that's what you want to do, I mean. If you aren't—"

"Oh, stop it, will you?" she demanded as she brushed past. "I wouldn't have brought it up if I wasn't hungry. We can't all have ice cream for dinner, you know. I have it on the best authority that I'm supposed to be eating blueberries and broccoli, not banana splits."

And they were back, just that easily, sliding into the familiar give-and-take relationship that he had grown so used to. That, he had realized when he was listening to Reece, he had come to depend on in the weeks Camille had been back in town.

"So, that's what you want?" He crossed to the fridge. "Blueberries and broccoli?"

"You're joking, but it doesn't sound all that repulsive to me."

"I'm going to pretend you didn't say that." He glanced at the shelves. "Well, we have the chicken I cooked earlier. I assume that burned smell lingering in the air is the vegetable stir-fry I'd started before storming out?"

"It is."

"All right, then. How about—"

"Fajitas." She shoved him aside, pulled out a couple of red peppers and an onion. "Cut up the chicken and I'll get these in the pan. I bought some salsa and tortillas when I was at the store earlier and some great guacamole. I know you've got *queso blanco* in here somewhere…"

"Are you sure—" He bit his tongue before he could ruin the fragile peace that was slowly building between them.

"Go ahead and say it." Her tone was amused as she piled her armload of ingredients on the kitchen counter. "You know you're dying to."

"It's nothing. Just, the books say that sometimes spicy food isn't the best thing for—"

"And sometimes the books don't know what they're talking about," Camille shot back, as she washed the peppers and then began slicing them in a series of quick, expert slices of the knife. "I had Thai food for lunch today and it was delicious."

He blanched at the thought of all the hot peppers and exotic ingredients that went into Thai cuisine. "It wasn't fish, was it? You know, there are a lot of fish with high mercury contents that pregnant women aren't supposed to eat. In fact, I have a list in the drawer next to the stove—"

"I know. I found it days ago. Now relax, Matt. I promise not to have any fun while I'm pregnant. Okay?"

He felt her words like a blow. "That's not what I meant. You're doing a great job, taking really good care of yourself. You think I don't know that?"

"Oh, lighten up, already. You take everything so seriously." She tossed him an onion. "Here, cut this, and we'll be eating in no time."

True to her word, Camille had the peppers and onions sizzling with a bunch of spices within a few minutes and his kitchen was filled with the fragrant, mouthwatering scent of homemade Mexican food. Within minutes, they were seated at the table, wrapping up tortillas filled with black beans, chicken, vegetables and guacamole.

They talked through dinner, but kept things light as if by tacit agreement. He told her of Justin and Johnny's bathtub submarine and she told him about her latest temp job at a pediatric dentist's office—and the little boy they'd had who had bitten the doctor every time she tried to put a finger in his mouth.

"You should have seen the boy's poor mother. She was so red I thought she was going to have a stroke."

"I bet. What did the dentist do?"

"Bribed him with everything she could get her hands on and when that didn't work, told the mother that he obviously had a strong set of chompers, which showed every appearance of being in working order. The X-rays looked fine, so she sent him on his way."

"I don't know how pediatric doctors do it," he mused. "Kids are so unpredictable and difficult, so—"

"Wonderful and unique." Camille's eyes met his across the dinner table. "Actually, of all the temp jobs I've had, that was the one I like the most."

"Really, even with kids like that?"

"Especially with kids like that. He wasn't malicious, just mischievous. And nervous—a dangerous combination, but not necessarily a bad one."

Her response surprised him even as it warmed him, had him thinking for the first time of what their own child would be like. Oh, he'd imagined the baby—sleepless nights, crying, cuddling—but nothing beyond that, nothing about when the baby turned into a toddler or a child, with his own personality. Now that he was thinking about it, the idea wasn't an unpleasant one.

Would their child have Camille's dark, wild curls or the thick auburn hair that had been the bane of his existence growing up? Camille's wild disposition or his need for order? Whoever it turned out to be, the child would probably inherit their artistic gifts, whatever it chose to do with them. He warmed to the idea of a son or daughter who followed in his footsteps, who joined the architectural firm he and Reece had worked so hard to build through the years.

"Hey, where'd you go?" Camille's voice drew him away from the might-bes and into the present.

"I don't know. Just thinking—about kids and the future."

Her eyes darkened to a wicked amethyst and her laugh was as smooth as the fifty-year-old Scotch Reece had gotten him for his birthday. "Trying to imagine our child biting some dentist?"

"Trying to imagine our child at all. And I was planning its future career path."

She raised a brow. "An architect, hmm?"

"Or an artist, like its mother."

"Somehow I doubt that's what you were imagining— our baby globe-hopping as he perfects his art."

"Maybe not our *baby*... But a twenty-year-old art student? Yeah. I can see him clearly. Living in a garret in Paris as he struggles for his art, with both of us sneaking him money to help him survive."

"Or her, posing as an artist's model for the petty cash, inspiring some other painter as she perfects her own craft."

"Is that what you did? *Do,* I mean?" He tried to disguise the intensity of his interest in her answer. "Model for French painters?"

"And Italian glassblowers and Dutch watercolorists and Spanish sculptors." She laughed, gestured at her stomach. "Or at least I did. Not much call for a model with a huge stomach these days."

"Your stomach isn't huge! You're barely showing."

"That's because you haven't seen me naked."

Her words hung between them, the three-ton elephant in the room, as he tried his damnedest *not* to picture her naked. Of course, it was impossible.

She'd always been beautiful—long, lean lines with sharp angles and narrow hips. But now, four and a half months into her pregnancy, she was gorgeous. Her breasts were fuller, her hips rounder. And the curve of her stomach, where she sheltered his baby? He'd spent more than one sweaty, lust-filled night thinking about what it would be like to kiss his way down the firmness of her growing belly to what lay beneath.

"No." He cleared his suddenly thick throat. "I haven't. Not lately, anyway."

Her breath hitched at his reply, her eyes darkening to the wild purple of the belladonna that used to grow in the woods behind his childhood home. Dark and dangerous and incredibly inviting, like the deadly nightshade of his youth, they promised things he knew weren't good for him. And yet he didn't care—in those moments all his careful planning went out the window and all he could think about was touching her.

"Do you want—" Her voice broke. "Do you want to touch my stomach? Feel the baby—"

"Yes!" At another time he might be embarrassed by the eagerness of his answer, but right now all he could think about was getting his hands on Camille's silky skin, about being close to her again after the weeks and months of being without her. He nearly knocked his chair over in his haste to get to her, his normal finesse abandoning him as all the blood in his brain rushed due south.

She laughed, a sexy, husky sound that made his nerves sizzle and his hands shake. Dropping to his knees in front of Camille, he kept his eyes on her face. Her cheeks were flushed, her eyes growing darker with each second that passed, and the tip of her tongue kept darting out to lick her lips in a rhythm that was driving him insane.

Slowly, so slowly that he could hear each rasp of the cotton against her skin, Camille lifted her tank top until it was right under her bra line. He wanted to groan, to beg her to take it off completely so he could see the ripe, round breasts that had been keeping him up at night, but even lust-crazed, he was smart enough to take what she was offering and demand nothing else.

Her stomach was the same golden cream he remembered, and memories of the last time he'd seen her stomach hung in the air between them. It was the night before she'd left him and he'd spent long minutes kissing her midriff, nuzzling and tickling and tasting as he worshipped her with his hands and lips and tongue.

Now, at this instant, he wanted nothing more than to repeat the experience.

"Can I—"

"Yes!" It was her turn to step on his words, to grab his hands with her own trembling fingers and bring his palms to rest on her stomach. At the first contact of his callused fingers to her smooth belly she gasped, then sighed, her entire body arching up for closer contact, firmer pressure.

He followed her lead, pressed his thumbs into the downward curve of her abdomen while his fingers stroked on either side of her navel. She groaned, shuddered, pressed herself even harder against his hands, and he nearly lost it. Nearly pulled her into his lap and took her in whatever way she would let him, whatever way he could.

But there was something soothing in stroking her belly—in feeling the firm resilience of his child beneath his palm, sheltered deep within her body—that gave him more than a quick sexual encounter would.

So he took his time, caressing every inch of her bared tummy.

Fondling each new curve and slope.

Petting over and around the sexy indentation of her belly button.

By the time he was done, she was shuddering and he was so aroused he could barely see. The air was bellowing in and out of his lungs, as if he had just finished running a marathon in record time, and he wanted nothing more than to kiss her.

But he didn't know the rules, didn't know how far she wanted to—

Camille leaned forward, giving him a fabulous view of her spectacular breasts, but then even that was forgotten as she claimed his lips with her own.

AT THE FIRST TOUCH OF Matt's lips on her own, Camille's world imploded. Reaching up, she tangled her fingers in the ends of his deliberately styled hair and tugged until he was up on his knees, his face nearly level with her own. Only then did she give herself over to the kiss and the feelings that were slamming through her body like tidal waves.

She might have initiated the kiss, initiated the contact, but Matt took over in the space of one heartbeat to the next. He was gentle, so gentle, as his lips moved against her own, teasing her, playing with her mouth much the same way his fingers had done to her stomach moments before.

His tongue licked over her lips, toying with the center indentation of her upper lip before moving on to the lush fullness of her lower one. He swept over the corners of her mouth, teasing her—tormenting her—before sweeping inside to taste her.

She wrapped her arms around him, pulled him closer as his tongue toyed with her own. He tasted like lemon custard and bittersweet chocolate, smelled of the earthy, saltiness of the ocean. She wanted to get closer still, wanted to wrap herself up in him until there was nothing between them but the silkiness of skin and the quick beat of their hearts.

Her fingers tightened in his hair and Matt groaned, deepening the kiss until his tongue was everywhere— sweeping over the top of her mouth, playing with the little bit of skin that connected her upper lip to her gum, tangling with her own tongue in a rhythm that set her on fire.

His arms closed around her, his fingers stroking her spine to cup the nape of her neck. She shivered at the touch, feeling vulnerable and powerful and sexier than she had since she'd left him all those months before. In the back of her mind, an alarm sounded—along with all the reasons this was a bad idea.

But her body was on fire, her sex aching with the need to feel Matt inside of her, and it was easier—infinitely easier—to just go with the desire. With the need. With the aching, yawning emptiness inside of her that called out for so much more.

Matt's hands slipped around to cup her face and his lips raced over her cheeks, down her jaw and the long line of her neck to the hollow of her throat. As he nuzzled her there, his tongue stroking her pulse points and the bones below them, she felt herself melt and knew that there was nothing she would refuse him now. Nothing she would deny him.

She tangled her fingers in the fabric of his T-shirt, shoved it out of the way so she could feel the burning heat of his back against her hands. Matt groaned again, nipped at her throat and she dug her nails into the muscular pads of his shoulders.

"Shit, Camille." He wrenched his mouth away from hers, took a series of huge, gulping breaths. "Are you trying to kill me?"

"Yes." She turned her head, found his mouth with her own, and moaned with the power and the pleasure that swept through her. "The same way you're killing me. I need you, Matt. I need you."

His hands fisted in her hair, yanked her head back, and then he was devouring her. His mouth was everywhere, everywhere, and she felt herself go up in flames. She whimpered, spread her legs until he was inside her thighs, his hardness pressed to the very heart of her. Then she started to rock.

Matt cursed again, tried to get control of his rampaging libido. But it was hard with Camille shaking and arching and whimpering against him, begging him for what he so desperately wanted to give her. He reached between them, rubbed over the damp cotton of her shorts. She moaned, her head falling back against the chair as her hips bucked against his hand, and he nearly came in his jeans.

She was so hot, so responsive, that he could barely hold himself back. But it wouldn't be right, he told himself. He was leaving for Tokyo tomorrow—for three weeks at least—and she deserved more than the quick *wham, bam, thank you, ma'am* that he was currently capable of providing. She deserved long, sweat-soaked nights and a lover who would be around to hold her in the morning.

He couldn't give her that, not now.

But at the same time, it would kill him to leave her like this—her body screaming for release as she wrapped herself around him.

Pulling back just a little, he slipped one finger inside the crotch of her shorts, her panties. Added a second, then a third, as her body vibrated like an arrow on a bow.

"Matt, please!"

"I know, sweetheart, I know. I've got you." Then he slid a finger deep inside of her, cursed again at the tight heat of her as she closed around him. He found her most sensitive spot, started to stroke. Once, twice.

"Matt, oh, please!" She grabbed his hair in her hands, pulled his mouth down to hers and bit him, hard. He tightened to the point of pain and beyond as he took her mouth with his own.

She clenched his finger, nearly had him seeing stars as he slid another one inside of her. He thrust his tongue deep into her mouth, stroked, then retreated, did the same thing again and again, mimicking the motion and rhythm of his fingers in her sex.

Her body was arching, thrashing, embracing around him as she rode his hand, and he wanted nothing more than to be inside her. Nothing more than to let her ride him the way she was riding his hand.

Knowing his control was at an all-time low, but determined to hang on to it, he swept his thumb around her clitoris in a rhythm he knew she liked. Around and around as his fingers and tongue thrust deep inside of her and his erection strained to be set free.

Suddenly Camille cried out, her legs tightening around his own as her body contracted rhythmically at his fingers. He thrust deeper, stroked just a little harder and nearly came himself as her orgasm overtook her.

She ripped her mouth from his, let her head fall back as wave after wave rippled through her. Her cheeks and the tops of her breasts were flushed a rosy, inviting pink and he wanted nothing more than to lean forward and take a bite of her. But she was still coming, her body holding on to his as if he was her only anchor, and he was loath to do anything to disturb her.

When it was over, when she'd finally floated back to earth, Camille leaned forward and wrapped her arms around Matt. "You didn't finish," she whispered in his ear. "Don't you want to make love?"

He laughed, a painful, grating sound, and pushed away from her. "I wouldn't feel right about it."

She gasped, felt as though he'd punched her with his careless words. With fumbling fingers, she yanked her tank top and shorts back into place, then stood up, wondering how soon she could make her escape.

Could she have been a bigger idiot?

"I'm leaving for Tokyo tomorrow, Camille."

Of all the things she'd been expecting him to say, that had been the furthest from her mind. Freezing in her headlong flight across the kitchen, she turned and whispered, "Tokyo?"

"Some problems have cropped up with a building that's going up there. Reece and I designed it and one of the firm's architects is already on-site. But they want a partner, so I'm on the first flight out in the morning."

"How long are you going to be gone?"

"Three weeks at least—maybe more, if I can't figure out a solution relatively quickly."

"Wow," she murmured inanely, wishing she could think of something more intelligent to say. But her knees were still shaking from the orgasm he'd given her and all she could really think about was the fact that she was going to miss Matt while he was gone.

Which was ridiculous, because she never missed anyone. Never let herself care about anyone enough to miss him or her.

But there was a definite hollow place inside her, one that told her Matt had somehow managed to worm his way past her defenses. That he had somehow managed to touch her heart when she'd been so careful, before him, to keep it guarded.

She wanted to believe it was the baby—the fact that he was her child's father—that was messing her up, but she was afraid it was more than that, and less. Afraid that it was just Matt, with his caring and concern and interminable schedules that had worked his way past all her usual roadblocks.

"I'm sorry." He crossed to her. "I know this is crappy timing and if I could get out of it, I would."

"No." She forced her brain back into gear, made herself smile through the bewildering mix of feelings churning inside of her. "Hey, I'm the last one to lay a guilt trip on you. Definitely, enjoy Tokyo—and send me a postcard. It's one of the few places I've been that I really want to go back to again."

He searched her eyes, his own brown ones warm with concern and the remnants of desire. "You see why I had to stop, right? I can't just make love to you tonight and then run out on you before dawn."

His words were so eerily reminiscent of what she'd done to him five months earlier—had fantastic sex and then bailed—that she couldn't look him in the eye.

Of course Matt couldn't make love to her and run—not with so much unsettled between them. It wasn't in his emotional makeup to hurt someone like that. It didn't make her special, but it did make her very, very lucky.

"It's no big deal," she said, working to keep her voice light. "I understand business. But if you want to come back to my bedroom with me now, the offer still stands."

His eyes darkened until they were nearly black, and the look he gave her was so smoldering her toes actually curled against the warm maple floors. She wanted to feel him inside her again, wanted to be the sole focus of Matt's enthusiastic and intense lovemaking at least once before he jetted off for Asia.

But then he shook his head, dropped a light kiss on her forehead before trailing his lips down her cheek to her mouth. "I would like nothing more than to come back to your room with you and spend all night reminding both of us how good we are together." He whispered the words against her lips, sent shivers down her back with each rasping syllable he spoke.

"Then come." She didn't even care that she was pleading.

"I can't. When I make love to you again—and believe me, that's the first thing on my agenda when I come back from Tokyo—it's not going to be a quick thing that doesn't mean anything. If we do this, Camille, then it's going to mean something—for both of us."

"Isn't that supposed to be my line?" Her attempt at humor fell flat between them.

"I would hope it was both our line. So think about it while I'm gone, decide if you can live with what I'm saying."

Sudden nerves shook her to her core, along with the knowledge that Matt meant exactly what he was saying. If they were together again he would want a commitment, would want her to admit that there was something more between them than good, old-fashioned lust. The fear such a thought brought on made her reply more flippantly than she would have liked.

"So you're saying you won't sleep with me unless you can respect me in the morning."

His mouth curved into the crooked grin she liked so much, but there was a bite behind it that had butterflies flapping in her stomach. "No, I'm saying I won't sleep with you unless *you* can respect *me* in the morning. It's a totally different dynamic."

It sure was, and one she wasn't sure she could live up to. Her uncertainty must have shown, though, because Matt leaned forward and took her mouth in a tender, emotion-filled kiss.

When he moved away, his normal grin was back in place. "Hey, don't look so worried. You've got almost a month to decide."

That's what she was worried about—and he had to know it. With a month stretching between tonight and their next meeting, there was no way she could claim—even to herself—that sleeping with Matt was an impetuous move. If she slept with him again—when she slept with him—she'd go into it with her eyes wide-open and no excuses about not knowing the rules. His plan was diabolical—and brilliant in its simplicity.

Grabbing one of the hard candies she'd recently grown to love out of the bag she kept stashed in the pantry, she headed out of the kitchen without another word. But when she got to the doorway that led to the family room, she shot a question over her shoulder. "So, do you need help packing?"

Though her back was turned and she couldn't see it, she could hear the grin that split his face at her words. "I thought you'd never ask."

CHAPTER TWELVE

CAMILLE WOKE UP FROM HER NAP on the couch to the sound of the garage door opening. Bolting upright, all she could think of was that Matt was back. With a huge grin, she jumped to her feet and raced for the garage. He'd been gone three weeks and she'd missed him so much, more than she'd ever missed anyone before.

Why hadn't he told her he was catching a plane when they had talked the day before? She would have made sure she had food in the house, that the sheets on her bed were clean. That she'd shaved her legs. Exhausted by work and the pregnancy, worn down by missing Matt, she'd let everything go these past weeks. And now she was paying the price.

But when she opened the door into the garage, it was to find a tall, curvy woman carting boxes from the back of her car into the corner of Matt's garage. "Can I help you?" she demanded, wondering who on earth the redhead could be and whether she should call the police.

"Hi." The woman plopped the box she was carrying on top of one she'd already brought in, then came forward, hand extended. "I'm Matt's sister, Rhiannon. You must be Camille."

Matt's sister? Camille stared at her dumbly for a few seconds, unsure of how to respond. What was she doing here—and why hadn't Matt warned her his family might stop by? Camille was dressed in an old, paint-stained T-shirt and a pair of maternity jeans—definitely not what she would have chosen to make a first impression. Rhiannon was dressed impeccably—in a pair of tailored trousers and a crisp, boyfriend-style blouse, and as Rhiannon's eyes swept over her, Camille felt the old feelings of insecurity rise up within her.

Who was she kidding? She didn't fit in here, not with Matt and not with his beautiful, glamorous sister. She wanted to turn tail and run, but with Rhiannon's outstretched hand all but in her face, she had little choice but to take it.

"Yes, I'm Camille. It's nice to meet you." She glanced over at Rhiannon's still-full trunk. "I'm sorry, I wasn't expecting company. Matt didn't tell me you'd be stopping by."

"He doesn't know. I just sold my house, and months ago Matt told me I could store some of my stuff in his garage, just until I get everything situated in my new condo. As I was packing up twelve years of stuff, I realized I needed to take him up on the offer." She held her hands out, palm up. "So here I am."

"Here you are." Camille stared at her incredulously, feeling even more out of place. Who packed looking like a fashion plate? And if this was what Matt was used to, what the hell was he doing with her?

Rhiannon turned back to unload another box and Camille belatedly remembered her manners. "Do you need some help?" She started into the garage.

"No, of course not! There aren't that many boxes and Matt would kill me if I let you lift something in your condition. Just forget I'm here—I'll finish unloading and then get out of your hair."

But as Camille watched her lift another box, Rhiannon's arms trembled with the strain. Or maybe it was exhaustion—looking closer, she saw the same dark circles under Rhiannon's eyes that she saw when she looked at herself in the mirror.

"I can carry some of the lighter stuff," she said firmly, making her way to the car.

"Camille, honestly, I'm fine."

"Just point me in the right direction. The sooner we're done here, the sooner you can come inside and have a glass of iced tea with me. I can't believe it's nearly fall and it's still this hot out."

Rhiannon laughed. "Don't you know, Texas only has two temperatures—hot and hotter."

"I'm figuring that out," Camille said as she tested the weight of one of the smaller boxes marked Fragile. It only weighed a couple of pounds, so she carried it carefully to the other side of the garage and set it on an empty shelving unit Matt had back there.

The two women worked in companionable silence for a few minutes and when the last box had been unloaded, Camille asked, "How about that iced tea?"

"I'd love a glass."

"Then follow me." Camille led the way into the kitchen, where she filled two glasses with the cold liquid and handed one to Rhiannon. "I'm glad you stopped by today," she said, as Rhiannon took her first sip.

"Me, too. I've been dying to meet you, but Matt hasn't been exactly forthcoming. I think he wanted to keep you to himself for a while before the horde of Jenkins women descended."

"Horde?" Camille kept her smile in place through sheer will alone. "How many of you are there?"

"Well, just the four of us in Matt's immediate family, but our aunts and cousins are just as anxious to meet you." She glanced down at Camille's stomach. "None of my sisters or cousins have kids, so this is the first baby to be born in the family in quite a while. Everyone's excited."

"I hadn't realized." Her heart was beating too fast and the walls seemed to be closing in. How many people had Matt told about the pregnancy, anyway? How big was his family?

"In fact, Mom and I were talking the other day and we would love to throw you a baby shower," Rhiannon continued, completely oblivious to Camille's discomfort.

"A baby shower?"

"Yes. It'll be so much fun. I'm a party planner by occupation, but it will be a blast planning something for family. That is, if you don't already have plans for a shower? If your friends are already planning to throw you one, I totally understand."

What friends? she wanted to ask. The ones who were scattered around the world, whom she only spoke to once or twice a year? Or the ones she hadn't spoken to for longer than that—they didn't even know she was pregnant.

"No. Nobody's throwing me a shower yet."

"Wonderful! Well then, we'll definitely plan on it." She whipped out her BlackBerry. "I figured sometime around the seven-and-a-half-month mark—which should be mid-October, right? Let me give you a few dates and you can tell me what works for you."

She rattled off some numbers, but Camille couldn't concentrate. October was weeks and weeks away—she never made plans that far in advance. Sweat that had nothing to do with the heat outside suddenly rolled down her spine. This baby was boxing her in a little more every day.

"Um, pick whatever date works for you. My schedule is pretty wide-open."

"Are you sure?"

"Absolutely. I can paint anytime."

"That's right—Matt told me you're an artist."

"I am."

"What do you paint, if you don't mind me asking?"

"I specialize in portraits, but I do some other stuff, as well."

"Really?" Rhiannon looked fascinated. "Portraits? You know, I have a client who's looking for a good portrait artist. Do you mind if I pass your name along? She's got lots of connections—if she goes with you, you'll probably get a lot of other work out of it."

More ties wrapping around her, keeping her here. Camille's heart was racing, but she did her best to ignore it. "That would be great, thanks." Maybe she could get the portraits done before the baby was born—then she wouldn't be any more tied down than she wanted to be.

"Fabulous." Rhiannon pulled out a business card and handed it to her. "So whenever you get a list together of people who you want to invite to the shower, e-mail it to me and I'll take care of all the invitations."

Camille froze in the act of taking the card. She'd assumed when Rhiannon had said she wanted to throw her a shower, it would be for Matt's side of the family. The idea that she was supposed to invite guests, too—she didn't have anybody to put on the list. Not one person.

"Um, maybe a shower isn't such a great idea. I've only been in Austin a couple of months and really don't know anyone well enough to invite them."

"Oh, don't worry about that. Matt has tons of friends—talk to him and I'm sure we'll end up with a huge list."

Once again, she was struck by the difference between her life and Matt's. His was filled with people—everyone from casual acquaintances to lifelong friends to a huge, extended family. What did she have? Two battered suitcases and a baby under her heart.

How could she possibly ever be enough for him? She couldn't—she'd known that months ago when she'd left for Rio and she'd known it when she'd come back to tell him about the pregnancy. But somewhere in the past few months, she'd lost track of it. She'd forgotten who she was, who he was and why the two of them really didn't mix.

For the first time, she wondered if she was just one of the horde. Just one more person that Matt had picked up as he went through his life. Someone who meant something to him—she was the mother of his child, after all—but not someone special. Not the way he was to her. She'd spent her life dodging entanglements and letting Matt in had been a huge step for her.

The same couldn't be said of him. He loved people, thrived on building relationships. Was she just one more in a long string of friends and lovers and family? Had she been a fool to open up, to think that maybe they had a chance to build something? The thought made her stomach hurt and suddenly she wanted nothing so much as for Rhiannon to leave.

Matt's sister must have sensed Camille's sudden discomfiture, because she quickly drained her iced tea glass and hopped out of the chair where she'd been sitting. "I've got to go—I have an appointment at the office in half an hour." She carried her glass to the sink. "But I do want to say, again, how thrilled I am to meet you. Matt is so excited about being a father and it's wonderful to finally meet the woman who's put such a big smile on his face."

"It's nice to meet you, too. Matt talks about his family often. He loves you very much."

Rhiannon's smile faltered for a second, but then she bolstered it up. "We love him the same way. And please, if you need anything while Matt's in Tokyo, don't hesitate to call. I'd be more than happy to help with whatever you need."

"Thank you. I appreciate that." Camille said the words as she showed Rhiannon out, even though she knew she would never call Rhiannon—or anyone else in Matt's perfect family. Not with her words still ringing in Camille's ears.

Matt is so excited about being a father. Not, *he's excited to be with you* or *he's excited about having you back in his life,* but *he's excited about being a father.* Of course he was—and if he had to take her to get the baby, then so be it.

She should have figured it out long ago. He had everything—why would he want *her* when no one else ever had?

For the first time in months her feet started to itch and she headed for her bedroom at close to a dead run. It would only take her a few minutes to pack and then she could be in the wind. Again.

And if the idea wasn't as appealing to her as it normally was, then she would just fake it until it was. Because one thing was for sure, after her conversation with Rhiannon, there was no way she could sit around here, cooling her heels and waiting for Matt to come home.

"So, what'd Rick say when you went to see him today?" Matt walked out of the busy meeting and closed the door behind him. The hallway was blessedly quiet—and empty—so he leaned against the wall and let Camille's voice wash over him.

He'd been in Tokyo for twenty-three days and wasn't set to return home for five more days, and it was killing him. Usually he relished the travel that came with building a world-famous architectural firm, but lately it was wearing on him. Tokyo was amazing, but he missed Austin. Missed his house. Missed Camille.

"He said I'm disgustingly healthy and that the baby seems to be doing well. My stomach is just the right size, the baby's heart rate is directly in the middle of the normal range and everything else is exactly as it should be."

"Good. I'm glad to hear that. Anything else?"

"The sonogram is set for three weeks from today— you'll be back by then, right?" She sounded wistful, almost as if she missed him, too. Closing his eyes, he pictured Camille as he had last seen her, in short shorts and a tank top, her rounded stomach poking out just a little bit, and felt desire swamp him, along with a desperate homesickness that was anathema to him.

"Definitely. So, are you planning on finding out the sex of the baby?"

"I don't know. I mean, how do you feel about it?"

He imagined a little girl with Camille's fanciful nature, a little boy with her black, corkscrew curls. "I want to know, if you do."

"Oh, thank God! I'm dying to know, but didn't know how you felt about it. I saw the most beautiful crib the other day—it's white and round and surrounded by posts that I can drape lace onto. It's totally impractical, but I thought it'd be a gorgeous bed for a little girl."

"Lace, huh?" he teased. "What happened to all those gender-neutral shades you were looking at before I left?"

"Oh, I'm still looking at them. But I can't help it— there's just something about all that lace that gets to me. It must be the hormones or something."

"I guess. You've never really struck me as a lace kind of girl."

"Except for my underwear, you mean?"

He nearly groaned out loud at the images her words evoked, and he was suddenly rock hard and ready to go. Not that it took all that much to get him revved up these days—it had been almost six months since he'd had sex, a fact his body was reminding him of regularly—and unpleasantly. But thinking about Camille in her underwear would turn him on at the best of times, let alone now, when he was miserable, alone and dying to get his hands on her.

"You did that on purpose," he accused.

"Maybe." She paused. "It doesn't hurt to remind you of what you're missing while you're gone."

"Believe me, I don't need reminding."

"I'm glad to hear that." She paused, took a deep breath that had his instincts going on red alert.

"What's wrong, Camille? Is it the baby?"

"No, I told you the baby's fine. I can feel it moving now and everything."

"Really? What's it feel like?"

She laughed. "Sometimes like a butterfly's wings deep inside me and other times…"

"Yeah?"

"Other times it feels like a rhinoceros tap-dancing on my bladder. But Rick swears to me that's normal."

"A rhinoceros is normal?"

"Yep, and it's only going to get worse. Or so he promises."

"Lucky you."

"Yep. Lucky me."

Again he heard the tension in her voice and it made him nervous. "Just spit it out, Camille."

"Spit what out?"

"Whatever it is you're trying to work up the nerve to say."

She laughed again, but she seemed on edge this time. "It's no big deal. I just wanted to let you know I'm going to go on a little road trip."

His heart stuttered, then plummeted to somewhere in the vicinity of his toes. "You're leaving?" He was glad he was leaning against the wall or he might have fallen over.

"No! I mean, not permanently."

"Not permanently. Okay." His heart began a tentative climb back up to its regular place. He worked to keep his voice normal. "So, how long are you going to be gone?"

"I don't know. A few weeks, maybe."

He thought of the ticket he'd booked five days from then, of the breakneck pace he'd set trying to get home to her as quickly as possible. "I see. Where are you going?"

"I'm not sure yet. I'd been thinking about a short trip to Mexico or Jamaica—"

He ground his teeth, bit back his instinctive protest about developing countries and pregnancies and the kinds of places she liked to stay at. He knew Camille— knew that when she traveled, she liked to get the local color, that she resisted staying in big hotels or resorts if she could avoid it.

He also knew if he made a big deal about it, she'd be twice as likely to go where he didn't want her to. She was contrary like that. But damn it, that was his baby she was carrying. He had a right to be concerned, to worry about its health and well-being. To worry about her well-being, too.

"But then I figured I should probably stick closer to home—for the baby's sake."

He blew out the breath he hadn't been aware he was holding, murmured a quick prayer of thanksgiving that she was showing more sense than he'd originally credited her for. "So where did you decide on?"

"I didn't. I'm just going to get in my car and drive. Where I end up is where I end up—it'll be fun. An adventure."

"You're just going to drive?" There he went again, sounding like the stupid parrot he always was when he was around her. But damn it, was she trying to kill him? This was craziness, absolute insanity.

"You don't have a plan or hotel reservations or a map?" He was proud of the fact that he managed to get all fifteen syllables out without raising his voice. "No one's expecting you anywhere?"

"Nope. Just me, a suitcase and the open road." Her voice was full of excitement at the new adventure, and he knew, in her head, she was already gone. "It'll be fun."

"Fun" wasn't quite what he'd call it. Still, he tried to keep his cool, tried not to tell her what an idiotic idea— "Camille, you can't do that!"

"Excuse me?" The excitement was gone, replaced by ice.

"It's not safe. A woman traveling alone, with no destination. Anything can happen. And are you renting a car or taking that death trap you've been driving?"

"There's nothing wrong with my car!"

He banged the back of his head against the wall. "Did you at least get new tires and an oil change? Take the car to a mechanic and get it checked over? If you break down in the middle of nowhere—"

"I'll deal with it, like I always do. I've traveled nine-tenths of the world on my own, Matt. I think I can manage a drive through the American South."

"Is that where you're going? To the South?" He thought about the 2010 hurricane season, which was right around the corner. Of the biker gangs roaming the interstates. Of a show he'd watched about numerous, mysterious disappearances along I-10 in the past few years.

"I just said I'm not sure where I'm going. I'll drive until I don't want to drive anymore."

"Yeah, that sounds like a great plan." He'd muttered the words, hadn't planned on her hearing them, but the sudden intake of breath on the other side of the Pacific told him he hadn't been as quiet as he'd thought.

"We don't all have to map out every second of our lives. I like being able to pick up and go wherever the mood takes me."

"You're almost seven months pregnant, Camille!"

"Believe me, I know that better than you. I'm the one with the swollen ankles and the weird cravings and I'm also the one who's starting to look like she swallowed a beach ball. So don't preach to me from halfway around the world about the fact that I'm carrying a baby."

"You're carrying *my* baby."

"And mine. And in less than three months, I'll be stuck in one place for God knows how long. So what's so wrong with me wanting to take off for a while before that happens? Before I have to give up everything."

"Is that how you see it? As giving up everything?"

"Isn't that how you see it? Both of our lives are changing, Matt."

"Yes, but look what we're gaining. A baby, Camille."

"I know that and I'm excited, Matt. I really am. And it's not like I'm taking off forever—I have to be back in Austin in three weeks for the sonogram, remember."

No, he hadn't remembered. Maybe he would have saved himself a lot of angst—not to mention a lot of backpedaling—if he'd remembered that one fact before going off the deep end.

But no, her uncertain return date wasn't his biggest problem with the whole cockamamy plan. It was the idea that she really thought getting in an old, unreliable car and traveling the country alone was a good idea.

"Matt?" Hiroko, the head of construction, stuck his head out of the conference room. "We're ready for you now."

"Yeah, give me a minute." He turned his back on the man.

"You need to go."

"I want to talk about this some more."

"There's nothing to talk about." Her voice softened. "I'll be fine, Matt. I promise. I'll take very good care of the baby."

"And yourself."

She laughed. "And myself."

"At least take my car."

"What? No! My car—"

"Is a disaster on wheels. If you're dead set on doing this, use my car. It's just sitting in the garage, gathering dust."

"Matt." Hiroko again. "They're getting restless."

He held up a hand. "Yeah, okay."

"Go, Matt! It'll all be good. I promise."

He gritted his teeth. "I'm going to hold you to that."

She giggled, and he could almost see the sparkle of her smile. "Take care of yourself, Camille."

"I will. And you take care of yourself." A soft *ssh* sound told him she had blown him a kiss. "Bye, Matt. See you in a few weeks."

"I—" But she'd already hung up. Flipping his phone closed, he headed back into the meeting room behind Hiroko. And fought the very uncharacteristic, very unprofessional urge to punch the nearest wall.

CAMILLE CRUISED DOWN I-10 into New Orleans, the top down on Matt's very cool BMW Roadster. She'd almost ignored him, had almost taken her own car, but at the last minute had put her suitcase in his instead. And she hadn't regretted it once. Man, this baby could fly!

She tried to avoid thoughts of Matt, of his obvious disapproval and the nearly overwhelming need she'd had to please him. When she'd hung up the phone, a part of her had already decided to stay, had figured a quick road trip wasn't worth the hassle of dealing with an angry, upset Matt.

Which was exactly why she'd left. After throwing a few outfits and some toiletries into a suitcase and turning off her cell phone, she had all but run out the door. No man was going to tell her what to do and there was no way she was going to stop doing what she wanted just because it made him unhappy.

Her one concession had been the car, but it wasn't as if it was a hardship. Pressing down on the accelerator, she zoomed around a couple of sedans, reveling in the freedom of the open road.

The air was thick as soup, hot and humid and redolent with the scents of the Deep South—magnolia blossoms, swamp water and chicory. It was an odd combination, but one she remembered from her own childhood, and she found a strange kind of comfort in that, though she would have denied it to her dying day.

It had been years since she'd been to New Orleans, even longer since she'd hightailed it out of town at seventeen, swearing never to come back. She'd broken that promise seven years ago, when her mother had died, and was breaking it again now, as she drove through Kenner, Louisiana, on her way to the French Quarter.

A lot had changed since she'd been here last—courtesy of Hurricane Katrina and the federal government. She found it amazing, and horrifying, that there were still abandoned cars by the side of the road; that molded-out, falling-down houses existed side by side with brand-new construction.

She cruised into downtown, swept down Canal amid lights and traffic and horns honking. In the distance she could hear music pouring into the streets from one of the many nightclubs the city was known for. New York might be the city that never slept, but the Big Easy was the city that never stopped partying. Every day was a brand-new adventure.

Functioning almost completely on autopilot, she turned onto North Rampart—the street that bordered the French Quarter to the north—and headed toward a little bed-and-breakfast that she remembered from her childhood. The price of a room was probably astronomical, but she was only planning on staying a couple of nights, if that. Especially since she wasn't sure what had driven her to New Orleans to begin with, when she'd set off from Austin with a vague idea of ending up in Nashville.

She shrugged and turned off the car stereo so she could hear the mixture of jazz and rock and zydeco floating out from the side-street bars, carried along by the thick air and steamy, nighttime wind. Already she was itching to go out, to immerse herself in the streets and bars and culture of her childhood, to grab her sketch pad and record the sights that had been her salvation when things had gotten bad at home.

She snorted, amended her thoughts. When things had gotten *worse* at home—they'd always been bad, but she'd only escaped to the Quarter when they'd become downright untenable.

Pulling to a stop in front of the B and B—it was still functioning as such, after all these years—she climbed out of the car and stretched. Then she went inside to check in.

Ten minutes later, both she and her luggage had made it to her third-floor room. The decor was charming, New Orleans French at its best. Pale yellow walls, sumptuous bedcovers, a toile-covered love seat and ottoman.

She yawned once, fought back a second one—along with the urge to curl up in her pretty bed and just go to sleep. The night was still young and the French Quarter was waiting. Besides, she was starving.

Taking a few minutes to splash water on her face and reapply some lip gloss and mascara, Camille slipped into her walking shoes and hit the door. There was no use changing—her maternity wardrobe was still incredibly limited, so the best she could hope for was another T-shirt and pair of jeans similar to the ones she was already wearing.

Though her stomach was growling—and the baby kicking in protest—she took her time walking through the streets, taking in the sights and reacquainting herself with a place that never changed. It was strange, eerie even, to walk these streets after fifteen years and find that everything had remained the same.

Pat O'Brien's was still doing a brisk business in hurricanes and piano music. The daiquiri stands still ran twenty-four hours, their frozen-drink machines loaded with alcoholic beverages of every color. Even the Jax Brewery was still standing, despite its close proximity to the water. The overpriced shops and restaurants that were the mainstay of the old building were thriving and she thought about stopping in for a minute, buying one of the pralines she'd loved as a child, but in the end she didn't want to stop her tour of the Quarter.

She wandered past Café Du Monde and the old French Market, toyed with the silk scarves and ribbons, the coffee beans and feathered masks, all the time immersing herself in the goods around her so she didn't have to think.

So she didn't have to acknowledge the memories that hovered just under the surface.

When she couldn't ignore her hunger any longer, she headed to the other end of Decatur and grabbed a bowl of French onion soup and a muffaletta from Café Maspero's, then wandered down to Jackson Square to watch the street musicians and vendors.

Settling herself next to an artist hawking watercolor street scenes of New Orleans, she pulled out her sketch pad and began to draw. It had been nearly fifteen years since she'd lined her own pockets with tourist dollars, selling her own wares right here against this same black iron fence.

It was amazing, really, how so much had changed for her in the past decade and a half—and so little. She slipped into the rhythm easily, sketching the horse-and-carriage ride cruising down Decatur, the carriage listing to one side, the horse old and tired. Then she moved on to the little boys with bottle caps on their shoes, tap-dancing for dimes and dollar bills.

More than once a tourist came up, wanted to see what she was drawing. She showed them, was surprised—and then amused—when more than one offered her money to draw a picture of him and his wife/lover/girlfriend. She accepted on a whim, and by the end of the night had made nearly two hundred dollars sketching tourists in front of Andrew Jackson's statue or the imposing St. Louis Cathedral that bordered the square to the north.

But even as she worked, her charcoal flying over the pad, she was aware of a yawning loneliness deep inside of her—a need to connect when there was no one around to really connect with.

It was the same loneliness she'd felt as a child, as a teenager, and it was humbling to realize she'd run for years, only to end up right back where she started from.

Part of her wanted to pack up right then, to run back to her B and B, throw her bag in the car and get the hell out of town as fast as Matt's car could carry her. But another part of her wanted to stay, was fascinated with how this whole trip was going to play out.

No one had been more surprised than she when she'd cruised through Baton Rouge on her way to the Crescent City, and now that she was here she couldn't help wondering what she was looking for. What she expected to find in this city where she'd experienced only pain.

Because she couldn't answer the questions—and because she didn't want to think too hard on them—Camille did what she always did. Pushed everything away and let the art take over.

Let her fingers fly over the sketch pad as the music and mayhem of the Big Easy flowed all around her.

Let the worries and the loneliness settle back, deep beneath the surface, where she didn't need to acknowledge them.

When the air finally grew quiet and the street cleaners rolled through the streets—sometime after 3:00 a.m.—she was still there, her charcoal crayon worn to a nub and her alienation more acute than ever.

CHAPTER THIRTEEN

MATT STEPPED OUT OF THE CAB, paid the driver and took his luggage from the trunk before slowly making his way up the driveway.

The house was dark, unwelcoming, and he cursed himself for those last kernels of hope he'd been holding on to all the way across the Pacific. That last little belief that Camille would have changed her mind, that she would be home waiting for him, not driving through the South with a bunch of Hell's Angels on her heels.

God, he'd wanted her to be home. Had needed her to be here when he got home. Over the past months, he'd gotten used to her being here—even if she wasn't the best housekeeper, even if she burned dinner more often than not, even if she exasperated him twenty-three hours out of twenty-four, he'd grown to appreciate her presence. To relish it, just as he relished the light she always left burning for him.

He was an idiot, he told himself, as he dragged his suitcase along the sidewalk that led to his front door. An idiot to have hoped that she would be here and a bigger idiot for thinking that her absence meant something other than the fact that she'd gotten restless feet.

She would be back. She'd promised. If not for him, then for the baby—for her doctor's appointment.

But for how long? That was the question. Leopards didn't change their spots. The old cliché—a favorite of his mother's—played through his head as he unlocked the door. The air-conditioning was off and he was hit by the dull, stale smell of a house that had been empty— almost as if Camille had been gone longer than four days.

But that was absurd, as was all this angst. There was nothing he could do about it, after all, and whining about it wasn't going to bring Camille back any faster.

Still, he was in a piss-poor mood as he deposited his luggage in his bedroom and headed to the kitchen for a snack—he'd been traveling for nearly twenty hours and he was starving.

How had this happened? he wondered as he reached into the fridge and found it empty save a few cans of his favorite beer. Again?

It wasn't like the last time, when he'd walked into the thing with Camille blindly, not knowing that he was going to fall for her when they were just supposed to be having fun.

This time he had known better. This time he'd been hyperaware, with both eyes wide-open. It was a kick in the stomach to realize it hadn't mattered in the slightest. After all the promises he'd made to himself, he was right back where he was almost seven months ago—alone, in love with Camille and waiting for her to realize that he meant more to her than a piazza in Italy—or a road trip in a convertible.

He'd been wrong about what he meant to her six months ago, and surprise, surprise, he was wrong again.

When had it become love? When had his attraction for her and interest in her and the baby become something more? Become everything?

He couldn't pinpoint the specific date—his feelings hadn't changed overnight, with a lightning bolt of emotion coming down from the sky to zap him. He'd been falling for her for quite some time, and it had been the little things that had sunk him.

Little things like the paint she often had smeared on her cheeks and down the side of her nose.

The blues she listened to at all hours of the day and night.

Her smile, with its shy little dimple and sunshiny sexiness.

There was so much more to Camille than he had originally thought, so much more than he had originally fallen for. She was smart and kind and funny and amazingly sweet underneath her acerbic exterior. She hated to say she was sorry, but she hated hurting someone more and always owned up to her mistakes.

But knowing these things about her didn't make her any easier to understand. Why was she so commitment-phobic? Who had hurt her so badly that it was easier for her to turn her back on love than it was to accept it?

Then again, maybe he was just seeing what he wanted to see. Looking for blame where there wasn't any. Maybe Camille was exactly what he'd originally thought her to be—a capricious butterfly, flitting from one adventure to the next without thought to the destruction she left in her wake.

Completely disgusted with himself—with his inability to resist Camille and with the self-pity he was all but drowning in—Matt popped open a can of beer and drained it in two long gulps. Then he stumbled, exhausted, into his bedroom and fell facedown onto the bed. Better to sleep than to try to figure out what made Camille tick. The latter was a waste of time, particularly as it wouldn't change anything. She was still gone and the house still felt sad and empty without her.

CAMILLE WALKED SLOWLY through the old iron gates, a small bouquet of violets clutched in her hand and a chip on her shoulder a mile wide. What the hell was she doing here? Why had she bothered to come, now, when she'd spent so long running from just this confrontation?

She took a few steps up the stone path, started to turn around nearly a dozen times before she made it to the huge magnolia tree at the fork in the trail. She had no business being here after all this time, should just turn around and go back to the B and B or the French Quarter. Should be anywhere else but where she was at this moment, standing here with her loneliness and fear clutched around her like a cloak.

After a two-day stay that had become five, she'd told the manager of the little bed-and-breakfast that she would be checking out in the morning. It wasn't too late to change her mind, to turn back and check out now. To continue on her road trip, far away from this city and all of its bad memories.

She'd actually turned around, had actually taken a few steps back the way she'd come, before common sense had reasserted itself. She was here now and if she left before doing what she'd come to do, it would always feel like she'd lost, not just the countless battles of her youth, but the overarching war, as well.

No, if she didn't do this now then she never would.

But as she stood in the shade of the giant tree, suddenly she couldn't get her bearings. It had been seven years since she'd last been here, seven years since her father had buried her mother in a funeral so pathetically small that the mourners hadn't even been able to ring the grave, one deep. He'd since died, was now buried beside her mother—or so the letter from her aunt had said. She hadn't made it back for the funeral, hadn't cared to mark his passing with anything more than a nod of acceptance—and relief that the bastard was finally gone and couldn't torment her anymore.

It was funny, really, how he'd never had time for her as a child, had never wanted anything to do with her when her mother was alive to bow and scrape for him. But the second he'd buried her mother—in the cheapest cement-block tomb he could find—he'd come looking for her. Had expected her to fall all over herself in adoration for him, as her mother had.

He'd left disappointed. After years of watching him mistreat her mother and ignore her, all Camille had wanted was for him to disappear.

Closing her eyes, she tried to recall her mother's funeral and the location of the grave. Was she supposed to go right or left? Stay on the path or take a turn through the grass toward the rows and rows of cement crypts at the back of the cemetery?

She turned to the right, stopped about halfway up the trail, and started sifting through the markers on the long brick wall. By the time she'd gotten through about half of them, her hand was shaking and panic was a wild thing inside of her. Her already shaky stomach fisted into knots and sweat dripped, cold and unforgiving, down her back.

Where was her mother? How had she lost her? Turning in circles as her breath came in giant gasps, Camille tried to calm down. To get control of herself.

But it was as if someone else had invaded her body—someone with more emotions than she had ever claimed to have. Trembling, breathing harshly, she ran her fingers over the remaining tombstones, only to be disappointed when she got to the end.

Where was her mother?

Standing in the middle of the cemetery, feeling as if she was the only person left on earth, Camille tried desperately to gain some control over her crazed emotions. But she was too far gone—there was a ringing in her ears, a roaring in her blood, a weakness in her limbs that she couldn't counteract.

With a plaintive cry, she fell to her knees on the hard rocks, her clutch of flowers scattering around her as she cried and cried and cried.

After the emotional storm had passed, and her tears dried up, she made no move to get up. Instead, she stretched out on the path and stared up at the overcast sky.

What had she been trying to prove by coming here, anyway? That her relationship with her mother hadn't been a total bust? That she wasn't completely alone in the world? That at some point, somewhere, someone had actually loved her?

How stupid could she get? she wondered, as disgust rolled through her. From the time she'd been old enough to understand what a family was supposed to be, she'd figured out that she didn't have one. Not really. Not like so many of the kids she went to school with.

Oh, her parents still lived together and she lived with them, but that didn't mean they'd had time for her, any more than it meant that they had loved her. For seventeen years she'd been expected to be seen and not heard—and not really seen, either, if she could avoid it. She'd made the unpardonable mistake of being born a girl and for that she would suffer interminably.

She'd worn rags, ill-fitted clothes her mother had found at the Salvation Army while her father dressed from the most exclusive stores. Had survived holiday after holiday, waiting for a present that never came while her father splurged on professional golf clubs. She'd waited and waited for him to notice her, to speak to her, to buy her a present—not because she wanted the things so much, but because she wanted some tangible proof that she mattered. That she existed.

That proof had never come—and it was a kick in the teeth to realize she was still waiting for it. That she was still that little girl who wanted nothing more than to belong to someone. To matter to someone.

She wasn't sure how long she lay there, working out the truth of her past and her present. Long enough, certainly, to figure out what she'd always known but somehow forgotten—that love was a gift and not to be taken lightly.

You couldn't make someone love you, but if they did, you should accept that love, hold on to it tightly, not throw it back in their faces like so much garbage.

Twilight was setting in when she finally climbed to her feet, the trees and rows of tombs casting long shadows on the fertile ground. With the panic gone and reason restored, the cemetery didn't look nearly as large as it had when she'd first arrived.

As she gathered the violets up, the location of her mother's grave came to her and she walked toward it with quick, sure steps. And when she found it, tucked modestly amid a row of five tombs, second from the bottom of the fourth column, she slid the violets into the small vase built into the stone marker. The flowers were a little ragged, a little worse for wear after her little meltdown, but she wanted to leave them anyway. A token for the mother who had never been able to see her in the shadow cast by her father.

They were her final goodbye—she wouldn't be coming back. Not to this cemetery and not to New Orleans.

Turning away, she hurried back to her car as fast as her pregnant body would let her. It was getting dark and she wanted to go home.

Home to Austin.

Home to Matt.

CHAPTER FOURTEEN

IT WAS EARLY MORNING and Matt was sitting on his couch, watching an early morning news show when he heard the electric garage door opener start to hum. He'd been home two days and hadn't been able to shake himself out of the morass of self-pity he'd been mired in since his last conversation with Camille, when he was in Tokyo.

He'd tried to call her a couple of times, but she hadn't answered—like that was a big surprise. Part of him was worried that something had happened to her, while the more cynical side of him said she was just being true to form.

Which is why when he heard the garage door go up, his first thought was that he was imagining things. Camille had only been gone for six days by his calculations, not nearly as long as she'd led him to believe. But when the garage door into the house crashed open and she called, "Matt?" he was up and heading toward the laundry room at a pace that was far from dignified.

"You're here!" she said, and her face was alight with such joy that it stopped him in his tracks. "I didn't think you'd have made it back from Tokyo yet."

"I got back two days ago." His voice was huskier than usual, but she looked so damned beautiful and he was so glad to see her that he couldn't stop emotion from clogging his throat, just a little.

"Why didn't you tell me when we talked? I wouldn't have taken off like that if I'd known you were coming back so soon." She threw her arms around him, pulled him into a warm, welcoming hug that had every inch of his body coming alive.

He pressed his face against her neck, reveled in the sweet scent of her and the feel of her safe and soft in his arms. "I thought you had restless feet."

"Only because it was lonely here without you. This house is too big for one person—I was freaking myself out rattling around in here by myself."

"I'm glad you came back." He squeezed her tighter and got a swift kick against his stomach for the effort.

"What was that?" he pulled back, astounded, stared at the hard lump of her stomach that had grown exponentially in the month since he'd seen her last.

"I told you, this baby is a future soccer star. It kicks really hard." She rubbed her belly for emphasis.

"Can I feel?"

"I thought you just did."

"You know what I mean." He placed a hand on her stomach, was shocked at how much harder it was than the last time he'd touched her. "Wow, you're really growing."

"Tell me about it. I feel like a beached whale half the time—I don't know how I'm going to make it three more months."

"You look absolutely beautiful."

"Yeah, right." She ran a hand over her hair self-consciously. "I've been driving your convertible for the past nine hours—'beautiful' isn't exactly what I'd call me."

"Well, then, you'd be wrong." He pressed on her stomach lightly, one finger at a time, as if he was playing the piano. "The baby doesn't seem to want to play with me." He was oddly disappointed.

"Give it a second. I can feel it moving a little—maybe it's just getting comfortable."

Just as she finished the sentence, he felt a powerful bump against his hand—followed by a second, then a third. "It's kicking me!"

"Of course it is. You think you're so special you don't deserve to share the wealth? Believe me, my bladder could use the break."

"It's so strong." He marveled for the second time. "I can't believe it."

"And only getting stronger, or so Rick says."

He glanced up at her and their gazes locked. Heat sizzled between them, turned his already aroused body into a seething mass of need. "I want to kiss you, Camille."

She grinned, a sassy little upturn of her lips that shot right to his heart. "I thought you'd never ask."

She tilted her head for his kiss, but he took his time getting there. If he was finally going to get her into bed after seven long months without her, he was going to make sure she was as hot as he was. And he was going to make it last.

Sliding his hands over her stomach to her hips, he glided them slowly up her ribs, pausing to let his thumbs toy with the soft undersides of her breasts. She gasped, her crazy violet eyes going huge and dark as he stroked her in a rhythm meant to soothe—and arouse.

"Matt." She whispered his name, but it could have been a shout the way it echoed in his head.

"Camille."

He moved his hands up a little farther, brushed his index fingers over her nipples. Once, twice.

Her skin flushed a delicate, rosy pink and her head lolled back, as if it had suddenly gotten too heavy for her to hold up. But when her eyes started to close, he cupped a hand under her chin and ordered, "Look at me."

Her lids flew open and her eyes were dreamy, unfocused. Leaning close to her, so close that he could feel her breath against his cheek, he demanded, "Tell me you want this, that you want me."

"I want you, Matt. That's never been in question."

He skimmed his lips over her collarbone to the curve of her neck. Inhaled her, trying to draw her so deep inside of him that he would never have to be without her again.

But as her words sunk in, he pulled back a little. "What does that mean?"

"What?" Her voice was little more than a rasp and her hands moved up his neck to clutch desperately at his hair. "Don't tease me."

"Sweetheart, you don't even know what teasing is yet. But you will, before tonight is over."

She moaned, arching so that her breasts brushed against his chest, and he nearly said to hell with it. Why was he drawing this out when he wanted nothing more than to be inside of her? Now.

Still, something about her last statement niggled at the back of his brain, wouldn't let him move on until he clarified it. "What did you mean, when you said that your wanting me had never been the question?"

She shrugged, looked away. "Can't we just make love?"

"Oh, we'll make love, Camille. That much I promise you. But I want to know what you meant, why you looked so sad when you said it."

She pulled away, wrapped her arms around her burgeoning stomach in a way that showed just how vulnerable she was feeling. "Camille? Sweetheart? What's wrong?"

For long seconds she didn't answer, just stared at him with those heartbreaking eyes of hers. But just when he was about to give up, to pull her into his arms and tell her that it didn't matter, she whispered, "Why do you want me?"

For a second he was sure he had misheard the question, then nearly laughed when he realized she was serious. "How could I not?" he asked.

"Because no one ever has."

He did laugh then. "Somehow I don't think you've been paying attention. From the moment I first laid eyes on you, I wanted you, Camille."

Her mouth turned downward. "You wanted my body."

"Of course I wanted your body." He reached for her, ran his hands down her long, graceful back. "What's not to want? But it's more than that. It was more than that then and it's definitely more than that now."

"Because of the baby?"

For the second time in as many minutes he tilted her chin up so that she was forced to look him in the eye. "Because of you. Camille, I want you because you're the most exciting woman I've ever met. You're talented and capricious and so beautiful that sometimes it hurts just to look at you.

"You make me crazy, but you also make me laugh. You make me smile on days when nothing else can. And you shake me up, pull me out of my plodding, plotting ways—show me that there's more to the world than schedules and plans. I have to work for every smile I get from you, but that's how I know they're genuine.

"Why do I want you?" he echoed her question. "Why on earth *wouldn't* I want you?"

For long seconds, she didn't do anything but stare at him with her amethyst eyes. Then, just as he'd decided she wouldn't respond, she whipped her tank top over her head and stood in front of him, in nothing but a lacy bra and maternity shorts.

Heat exploded inside of him, both at the sight of her and at the vulnerability she was showing. He knew she was uncomfortable with the changes in her body—he could see the uncertainty where before there had only been confidence, frivolity. But to him, she was just as lovely as she'd ever been—more so, really, with his baby growing inside of her.

Things had started as a game between them six months ago, but that had changed when he'd fallen for her. Changed again when she'd gotten pregnant. The game had taken on a life of its own, and now they were both more exposed—more emotionally naked—than he'd ever expected them to be.

And still it wasn't enough for him. He wanted all of her exposed to him—every inch of her gorgeous, feminine body.

Every emotion in her guarded, generous heart.

Every thought in her agile, interesting mind.

He wanted it all. And now, for this one moment, knew he would do whatever it took to get it.

Without taking his eyes from hers, he pulled his shirt over his head. Unfastened his jeans and let them—and his boxers—fall to the ground at his feet. He stood before her more vulnerable than he'd ever been in his life, and hoped she understood what he was offering.

Camille walked toward him slowly, her arm outstretched as if she couldn't wait to touch him. But then, when she was mere inches from him, she stopped. Let her hand drop back to her side. Slowly shrugged out of her bra, then shimmied her shorts and panties down her legs until she, too, was completely nude.

The sun had risen fully at some point during their little game, and her skin shone like fire in its sparkling rays. Her wild, crazy curls tumbled over her shoulders in ebony waves and her ripe, rounded body urged him forward like a siren's call.

Hunger rose in him—sharp, hot, all-encompassing—and he wanted nothing more than to take her with all the pent-up need he had inside him. But after so long, she deserved more than that—and so did he. He would take it slow with her—savor her. Then maybe, just maybe, it would be enough to calm the fire raging within him.

Pulling her into his arms, he kissed her until he was drowning in her.

Kissed her until he didn't know where she left off and he began.

Kissed her until she felt the same way.

He wanted her on fire, wanted her burning with the same need that threatened to eat him alive. He wanted to slip past her defenses, to see every secret part of her. He wanted—just once—for her to trust him enough to lose control.

He *needed* her to lose control, to let him inside of her. As he skimmed his lips over her razor-sharp cheekbones and down the delicate skin of her jaw, the world around him began caving in. He wanted her arms around him, her body beneath him, wanted to take over every part of her so that he knew that she was his.

So that she knew it, too.

Reaching for him, Camille cupped his face in her hands and brought his mouth back to hers. The second their lips met, he gave himself over to the conflagration gathering between them, around them.

With a groan, he slid his tongue inside her mouth, thrusting between her lips the way he wanted to thrust between her thighs. Demanding more and more from her, demanding all that she had to give.

CAMILLE WHIMPERED AT Matt's blatant invasion—his blatant claiming—and tried to pull away, to regroup. But he refused to let her go, his tongue stroking every inch of her mouth. His chest pressed against hers. His arms held her tightly to his long, lean body, so that her stomach was pressed firmly against his own.

Need raced through her—it had been so long since she'd held him like this. So long since she'd been held like this.

Tangling her tongue with his, she sucked him fully into her mouth and stroked the bottom of his tongue with her own. He growled deep in his throat while his hands twisted in her hair, holding her face to his.

Camille relinquished his tongue with a moan, tilting her head back until she could see his face. Until their eyes once again met. His were so dark that the pupils had disappeared, so deep that she swore she could fall in and keep falling.

But wasn't that what she'd already done, all those months ago? Fallen for him when she'd promised herself she wouldn't? Fallen for him despite the risk that came with caring for someone?

Usually, the threat of that kind of pain was enough to get her to back off. Enough to let her believe that she didn't need to be held. Didn't need to be loved.

As she looked at Matt in that moment—at the tenderness and the desire that existed side by side on his face— she knew that she'd been lying to herself all along.

She didn't want to pretend anymore. Didn't want to get up in the morning and tell herself that it was better that she was alone. For a while it had been better, but not now. Not with Matt in her life.

While she'd lain in that cemetery yesterday afternoon, she'd seen the path she was creating for herself—and it was nowhere she wanted to be. She had a baby on the way and a man she cared about more than she had ever cared about another human being, and for once she wasn't going to run. She would take a leap of faith, would grab on to the future she wanted with both hands and see where it took her.

Looking into his eyes, she promised herself that she wasn't going to run anymore. Matt was everything she wanted and more than she deserved and she would not turn her back on what they had simply because she was scared.

Suddenly, she was in a huge hurry, but Matt seemed almost hesitant, as if he was afraid to hurt her with her new, unwieldy body.

Determined to change that, she smiled sexily and murmured, "I won't break, you know. I'm still the same woman I was six months ago."

It was all the invitation he needed. Breathing harshly, he backed her up against the glass door that led to the backyard and held her there as his lips ran over her neck and shoulders and the hollow of her throat.

Fire raced through her wherever he touched, and she could tell he felt the same way. His breathing was harsh, his muscles tight, his arousal hard where it nestled in the juncture of her thighs.

And he was staring at her, watching her, with eyes of melted chocolate. She glanced down, suddenly over-whelmed by the need to see herself through his eyes. To understand what made him lick his lips while he gazed at her, to know why he was so aroused by this new shape of hers.

Her breasts were full, swollen, her nipples bright pink and hard as rubies. Her skin was pale, the dark blue veins of her breasts evident beneath the oh, so delicate skin. Her stomach jutted out beneath them, round and hard and ungainly, but he didn't seem to mind, his hands racing over the taut skin as if it was the most beautiful thing he'd ever seen.

His hands moved up, cupped her breasts, and she gasped at how good he felt.

"Are they sore?" he whispered, bending down to trace the upper curve of her breast with his mouth. "The books say—"

"Not too sore. Not if you're gentle." Her hands covered his, squeezed, in a plea for him to touch her. Really touch her.

"I will be. I promise." His tongue licked over her breast—softly, sweetly, tenderly. Tears sprang to her eyes at the care he was taking with her, but she blinked them back. She wasn't going to break down—not this time. No matter how cherished he made her feel.

Then his mouth turned rougher; darkness and flames licked their way from her nipples to her stomach, down her arms and legs, until they coalesced in the ache between her thighs.

"Matt, please." She thrashed against him, bucking and arching as she tried to coax him into giving her what she wanted. What she needed.

He only laughed and pulled his mouth away completely, his breath a soft breeze over her achingly aroused flesh. She grabbed his head in her hands, her fingers tangling in his silky, too-long hair as she tried to force his mouth back to her distended nipple.

"Don't tease me," she pleaded as she arched against him.

"Baby, I haven't begun to tease you." He curled his tongue around her areola, sucked it into his mouth with a power so strong he had her gasping.

"Too much?" he demanded, immediately softening the pressure.

"No, no, no!" It was a chant, a plea for him to continue. When he did, the pleasure was so intense she had to bite her lip to keep from screaming.

"Take me." She didn't care that she was begging, didn't care that she sounded hot and needy and completely overwhelmed. The only thing she could think about was getting Matt inside her, and she would do anything to get him there. Risk anything to have him where she so desperately needed him.

"That's what I'm doing." His breath was hot against her breast, his hair cool against her neck and chin. She was pushing against him, whimpering, pleading with every weapon she had for him to put her out of her misery.

He refused to be hurried, no matter how restlessly her legs moved against his or how desperately her hands clutched his hair. He pushed her and pushed her, licking delicately, nibbling softly, until she was on the brink of sobbing. Only then, when she was strung tight and on the edge of madness, did he drop to his knees in front of her.

"Oh, please!" She couldn't stop the whimper that welled in her throat, any more than she could keep from twisting the auburn hair in her suddenly tight fists.

Rough hands parted her trembling thighs, and he stared at her with burning, intense eyes. "You're so beautiful, Camille. So unbelievably beautiful." He reached one callused finger out and stroked right down the center of her.

She trembled again, his words and touch arrowing through her brain to her heart and onto her sex in one burning line. No man had ever looked at this most private part of her and called her beautiful before. No man had ever stared at her as if it was agony not to be inside her. No man but Matt.

The thought made heat explode within her, shooting her arousal from hot to feverish to downright frenzied. She could feel an orgasm welling powerfully within her and she stood there, shaking, while he brought her right to the brink with almost no effort at all.

"I like this," he murmured, leaning forward so his mouth brushed against her bare inner thigh and the small butterfly tattoo she'd gotten several months before. "It's new."

"I got it in Brazil."

He nuzzled the small tattoo, licked it. "It suits you," he murmured, running his lips over her hip bone and abdomen. As he stopped to nibble at each birthmark and freckle, she was deathly afraid that her legs would give out beneath her.

"Matt, I'm going to fall." Her hands clutched his shoulders.

"I won't let you." His mouth closed softly over her navel, his tongue incredibly gentle as it probed her belly button and the soft skin of her abdomen.

And then he was moving on, moving down, his lips skimming over the curve of her stomach, down the side of her hip. His tongue made little forays underneath her hip bone, delicate little touches that lit her up like a Roman candle. Sharp little nips that had her gasping for air.

"Matt." It was a cry of agony, a plea born of desperation, and his hands clenched her thighs as he realized just how far he had pushed her.

SHUDDERS RACKED MATT'S BODY as he buried his face between Camille's thighs. She smelled delicious, like brown sugar and vanilla and sweet, sweet strawberries.

He paused for a minute; simply absorbed her smell into himself. He took a deep breath, then another and another, while his thumbs stroked closer and closer to the slick folds of her sex.

With each slide of his thumb, she trembled more. With each clasp of his hands, she took a shuddering breath. And when he moved forward, blowing one long, warm stream of air against her, she started to cry, to sob, her body spasming with even the lightest touch of his against it.

He was on fire, his erection so hard that he feared he might explode if he didn't take her soon. But he wasn't ready for it to end, wasn't ready to send her careening over the edge so he could follow behind.

He wanted to savor her, to push her, push himself, higher than they'd ever gone before.

But she was coming apart, her body so sensitive and responsive that it humbled him even as it made him sweat.

"You're unbelievable," he muttered as he delivered one long lick along her gorgeous sex. "So incredibly responsive I could just—" He stopped talking as Camille screamed, her hands clutching his hair as flames ripped through her. He kissed her a second time, and then a third, lingering on her most sensitive spot.

She sobbed as she hurtled over the edge, orgasm roaring through her body like a series of shooting stars. He held her while she came, stoking the flames higher and higher until she was screaming silently, her hands clutching his shoulders in an effort to pull him up and into her.

Her need sent him over his own edge, and he stood in a rush. "I need to be inside you," he growled, as he turned her and pressed her front against the cool glass door.

Skimming his mouth over her neck, he reached between her legs to make sure that she was still ready for him. She was slick, swollen and so hot he shuddered with a desperate need to be inside her.

With a groan, he pulled her hips back, one of his hands cupping her stomach for support. And then, with his knees shaking and body throbbing, he sank into her, slowly.

She felt amazing, smooth and silky and so hot he feared she would burn him alive——but what a way for him to go. With her wrapped around him like a fist, her strong body quivering against his, he wanted nothing more than to stay like this forever. Working his way inside her as she had found her way inside him. Taking her as she took all of him.

Camille moaned as Matt entered her, shocked at how good he felt inside of her. At how much it felt like she finally, truly, had come home with him wrapped around her, sheltering her. Arching back, she tried desperately to get closer to him.

He held her steady, his thrusts more gentle than she'd expected from him, certainly more gentle than he had ever been before, and she struggled to find her voice.

"It's okay," she gasped, pressing her bottom into his stomach. "You won't hurt me."

His only answer was a low, deep groan as he thrust and retreated, thrust and retreated. Taking her with more care and reverence than he could have imagined possible.

"Matt," she gasped. "Please."

He pressed forward, then rested his cheek against her temple. "Is this okay?" he asked through gritted teeth, his breath coming in harsh pants against her ears. "Am I hurting you?"

"No, no, no!" She answered in a series of tortured gasps, so turned on by the care he was taking with her that she would have fallen if he hadn't been there to support her. She was trapped between a rock and a hard place—the stationary, unyielding door at her front, and his strong, immovable body behind her. She was trembling, shaking, barely able to hold herself up.

And then she didn't have to, because he was there, supporting her—his body an exquisite pressure within her own. He began to move—slow, tender thrusts that glided him in and out of her. The pleasure built and built until she was once again on the edge.

With the last of her waning strength, she pulled him against her as hard as she could, wanting him as deep as he could go.

He wasn't expecting it, and the move broke his composure, his unbelievable control. He went over the edge, took her with him in a powerful maelstrom of emotion and ecstasy that hollowed her out.

In those moments, Matt was all around her, inside her. Not just in her body, but in her mind and heart and soul. She felt the past melting away, the future—bright and bold and beautiful—coalescing within her, filling her up.

The sensations kept coming, never-ending waves of ecstasy that shot up her spine, her arms and legs, through every part of her. In a small part of her mind, she was conscious of him stiffening against her, of his body jerking inside hers while he came in a series of long, beautiful pulses.

When it was over, he didn't collapse on her as she'd expected. As she'd craved. Instead, he leaned down and swept her feet out from under her, cradling her against his powerful chest. Then he moved through the house to his bedroom, where he laid her gently on the navy blue comforter. He joined her, ran his hands over the taut skin of her stomach.

"I didn't hurt you—or the baby?"

"Oh, no. Not at all." She took his hands in her own, brought them to her mouth and kissed him. "It was the most amazing experience of my life."

"You're amazing," he said as he trailed kisses over her shoulder and down the slope of her arm. His voice was gravelly, rusty, as if it had been too long since he'd last spoken.

"You don't have to say that," she answered, rolling to her side and pulling her knees up to her beach ball of a stomach, so she wouldn't feel so exposed.

"I don't *have* to say anything." He ran a hand through her hair. "But that doesn't make it any less true."

With a smile, she pulled him into her arms and reveled in the feel of his big, warm body against her heart— reveled in what it felt like to finally come home.

CHAPTER FIFTEEN

THEY SPENT THE DAY IN BED, cuddling and making love and laughing about unimportant things. When she was hungry, Matt whipped up a couple of omelets, then dragged her outside with him to eat on the patio.

His house was on a hill overlooking the lake and they watched the sun set over the water as they debated baby names. "If it's a girl, I think we should name her Miranda," Camille suggested. "Or maybe Karina or Serendipity."

Matt choked on his water. "You want to name our child Serendipity? Not in this lifetime."

"Why not? It's a cool name. Plus, she'll be totally unique."

"Yeah, well, unique isn't exactly what all kids dream of being—especially in junior high."

"Is that bitterness I hear?"

He laughed. "Not on my part. My oldest sister had a rough time in school."

"Because of her name?"

"Partly. *Rhiannon* is no picnic for a thirteen-year-old, but it was a lot of stuff. Suffice it to say, she was unique and that wasn't appreciated by her peers."

One look at Matt's face told her Rhiannon's suffering hadn't stopped when she'd graduated and she wanted to ask him about it, but he had huge no-trespassing signs posted, so she let it go. "Okay. No Serendipity, then. How about Karina?"

"How about Lucy?"

"Eeew! No!"

"Okay, then. Maybe we should talk boy names."

"Maybe. How about Jacob?"

"Actually, that's the name of Reece's little boy. He was born a few weeks before you came back."

"Gabriel? Caine? Adam?"

He burst out laughing. "What's with the Biblical names?"

"I don't know. I guess I like them because they're strong. Filled with tradition."

"This from a woman who wanted to name her daughter Serendipity? Isn't there some middle ground, somewhere?"

"Matthew Jr.?"

"No. Definitely not."

"Why not?"

"Because I don't need to prove my manhood by saddling my son with my name. He can be his own person."

"Unique, you mean?"

"Ha-ha."

"Maybe we should wait until we find out its sex before we argue names." She moved to the swing he'd installed the summer before, sat down and began to slowly rock back and forth. "Look at this sunset. Isn't it gorgeous?"

"Absolutely."

"You're not even looking at it."

"I'm looking at something better."

Camille felt her cheeks warm. "Laying on the charm, Matt? I thought you'd figured out I was a sure thing."

He sat beside her, pulled her against him. "Is that what you think I'm doing? Trying to charm you?"

"No. I don't know. Maybe." She paused, then asked, "What *are* you doing?"

"Admiring the mother of my child."

"Ah, yes. Because hippos are quite the standard in beauty these days."

"Why are you so down on yourself? You look fabulous pregnant."

"Oh, I don't know. Maybe because it would be nice to get out of bed in the morning without having to roll off the edge."

He laughed. "You don't have to do that."

"Yeah, I do. Seriously, most mornings I flop around like a beached whale trying to find its way back to the water."

"Do you mind?"

"What?"

"Being pregnant? All the changes that you're going through, all the adjustments you're going to have to make."

"No, not really. I mean, in two more months I'll be back to normal. At least I hope so."

"I don't just mean your body. What about the fact that you'll be stuck in Austin, that your whole globe-trotting life will change."

"Globe-trotting life?" She giggled. "I'm not exactly Paris Hilton, you know."

"That's not what I meant."

"I know. But things don't have to change completely, right? I mean, I'm not really stuck here. I can leave anytime I want."

Matt felt himself freeze at Camille's words, at her calm acceptance that she wouldn't be stuck in Austin forever. But what had he been expecting—her to change just because they'd made love?

"Hey." She twisted in the seat to get a better look at him. "You've gone awfully quiet."

"Just thinking."

"Well, do you think you could think about some ice cream? I'm still a little hungry."

"Sure, let me go see what we have."

"I think there's some triple chocolate chunk in there— I bought it before I went to New Orleans."

"Triple chocolate chunk. Got it." He stood up. "I'll be right back."

As he headed into the kitchen, he shoved Camille's words out of his head. There was nothing he could do about them, so there was no use ruining the rest of the day worrying. If there was one thing he'd learned six months before, it was that Camille was going to do what Camille was going to do and he really didn't have a say, one way or the other.

The baby was crying. High-pitched, pathetic wails that were just getting louder the longer they went on. Feeling like he was swimming through pea soup, Matt struggled toward consciousness. *He had to get to the baby, had to—*

He woke up with a start, with a foggy brain and a too-fast heart. Drawing a deep breath into his lungs, and then another, he slowly got his bearings. Realized the only baby crying was in his mind.

He was wrapped tightly around a still-pregnant Camille, his hand resting on her swollen stomach. Beneath his fingers the baby squirmed and kicked. For the first time, its movements didn't reassure him.

He glanced at the clock on the nightstand—it read six forty-five. They'd been asleep nearly seven hours. Strange that it barely felt like two.

Careful not to wake Camille, he rolled away from her and sat up, planted his feet firmly on the floor. He told himself to just go back to bed for an additional hour, but he was still shaky and needed a couple of minutes to get himself together. In his head, he could still hear the baby sobbing.

Was this what he was letting himself in for? Matt wondered as he got up, yanked on a pair of sweats. Letting his baby in for? The two of them wanting—and waiting for—a woman who craved freedom more than she did them? It was an uncomfortable thought, but one he could no longer dodge.

I'm not really stuck here. I can leave anytime I want. Her words from the previous evening came back to him, as they had numerous times since their conversation on his patio. And they didn't sit any better now than they had the first time he'd heard them.

In fact, they sat worse.

Is that how she saw their relationship? The life he wanted to build with her and the baby? As being stuck?

After everything that had passed between them, they were right back where they'd started and it wasn't a good place to be.

He was sick of it. Sick of trying to please her. Sick of trying to hold on to a woman who didn't want to be held.

He'd even slept with his arms wrapped tightly around her, as if his subconscious was afraid she would bolt the first chance she got. He couldn't do it anymore.

Didn't want to do it anymore.

He headed down the hall to the kitchen, put on a pot of coffee. Then went outside to his patio and stared hard at Lake Travis.

He loved Camille. He really did—he'd known it six months ago when he'd asked her to stay and he knew it now, as surely as he knew that it was his baby she was carrying. But sometimes love wasn't enough. It hadn't been enough for his parents, hadn't been enough for Rhiannon and her husband, and it wasn't enough for him, either. Not now, not with Camille.

Maybe if the baby wasn't on the way, if he wasn't concerned about providing a stable home for his child, he could just go with it. Let her jerk him around for a few more months or a few more years as she flitted from place to place, never settling down. Never putting down roots.

But there was a baby on the way and that baby did need stability. And, he admitted to himself as he watched the first boats cross the lake in the early morning light, so did he.

He didn't like change, didn't like flying by the seat of his pants, but he would live with it if it meant he could have Camille. But he would never really have her—he could see that now. She would always be looking for the next great adventure, the next new thing. For him, loving her was adventure enough. But he could never be what she needed.

He stood out there for a long time, watching the boats go by, their sails shifting with each new gust of wind. Their courses changing on a whim of fate. Of serendipity. Eventually he heard her moving around in the kitchen, fixing a cup of coffee for herself.

He didn't go in to join her.

"Hey, you." Camille's arms wrapped around him from behind, her belly poking at his lower back. He closed his eyes, savored the feel of her against him for one second, two. Then slowly moved away from her warmth.

"Hey, yourself. Did you sleep well?"

"I did." Her smile was nearly blinding. "Do you know what I was thinking when I was brushing my teeth—that we should go on a picnic today. I know, it's Monday and you probably have to work, but you were in Japan for four weeks. Surely that buys you a little time off, doesn't it?"

"I have a couple of meetings today."

"So cancel them." She crossed to him, brushed a soft kiss over his lips. "Come on, Matt, you know you want to."

He stiffened, annoyed beyond measure at her simple request. "I can't just blow these people off, Camille. They're clients and they expect to see me."

"Okay, then. How about a picnic dinner? Can you get off a little early? I'll make something nice and we can go down to the edge of the lake and—"

Because he could almost see the romantic meal, he was harsher than he needed to be when he said, "I don't think that's a good idea."

"Oh." She reared back at his tone, forced a smile that didn't quite reach her eyes. "Okay, then. Maybe some other time."

As she headed back into the house, she asked, "What do you want for breakfast? I'm starving, as usual, so I thought I'd make some blueberry pancakes and—"

"Camille, don't."

Even the fake smile faded. "Don't what?"

"I know it's been more than two months since you moved in, but since I was in Tokyo…" He took a deep breath, tried not to feel like a total heel when he said, "I don't think this is working out. I think you should move out."

CAMILLE FROZE, CERTAIN for a minute that Matt couldn't possibly have said what she heard. Not after spending most of yesterday making love to her and cosseting her. He couldn't possibly have just told her to leave.

But the look on his face was grave, his behavior since she'd woken up indisputable. Still, she couldn't believe it. "You don't mean that. You *can't* mean that."

"I'm sorry, but I do."

"But why? I don't understand. After yesterday…"

"Yesterday was great."

"Yet you want me to move out? What, is it your turn to blow me off, because of what happened before?"

"No! Of course not."

"Then what is it?" She wanted to cross to him, to hold on to him, to make him tell her that this was all just a joke. A mistake. Something other than the complete and total devastation of the dreams she'd just begun to have.

"We don't want the same things."

"How do you know that? We haven't even talked—"

"Give me a break. We've done lots of talking these past months, maybe too much talking. You want a life that I can never be part of, a life that I'm afraid the baby won't even fit into."

"That isn't true." She took a deep breath, tried to fight the sickness that was rising up within her. It was more than nervousness, more than panic—it was a terror that was so acute that she was actually physically nauseous with it. "I love you, Matt. I know it's taken me too long to say it. I know I've been selfish and irresponsible and afraid, but I want to be with you, want to raise our baby with you. I'm still scared, but I want to try. Can't we at least try to be together?"

For a minute it looked as though he was softening, as though her words were getting through to him. But in the end, he closed her out—as thoroughly as she had once done to him. "I'm sorry. I am. But I can't do this. Not now. Not ever again. I don't love you—I *won't* love you. I need you to leave."

She didn't know what to say to him, couldn't think of anything *to* say as his words ripped through her like the sharpest of knives. But in the end her silence didn't matter—he had enough words for both of them.

"I mean, obviously I'll give you time to find an apartment. Take however—" his voice broke, but he continued on anyway "— long as you need. I understand that it isn't easy to find one now, with the college students just back—"

"Go to hell." She stumbled backward, nearly hit her back against the sliding glass door.

He swore, reached for her. "Be careful."

"Don't touch me!" She jerked away, slammed the door open and ran inside.

"Camille, don't do this. Please." He followed her. "I swear I'm not trying to hurt you. I just don't see how this can work out between us."

"I get that. Really. You don't need to keep saying it." She rushed headlong toward her room. "Don't follow me."

"But—"

"Don't. Follow. Me." Her door slammed after the last word, leaving him standing there, staring after her, and wondering if he'd just made the worst mistake of his life.

CHAPTER SIXTEEN

CAMILLE LISTENED AS THE GARAGE door opened, then closed a couple of minutes later, signaling that Matt had finally left for work. She rose carefully from the side of the bed where she'd been sitting, feeling as if one wrong move would shatter her. Part of her thought the concern superfluous—she already felt as though she'd fractured into a thousand little pieces.

Moving slowly, she opened up the suitcase she'd taken to New Orleans—it was already half-full, as she hadn't bothered unpacking it the day before. Crossing to her closet, she pulled out her meager supply of clothes and stuffed them in the suitcase. Then opened a second suitcase and filled it with everything else she owned—shoes and jewelry, toiletries and sketch pads.

Within ten minutes she was done. She still needed to gather her paints and canvasses, but that would probably take her a second trip. Her car wasn't big enough to carry everything.

As she rolled her suitcases down the stairs, her emotions threatened to choke her, but she bit them back. Tears were too small a bandage to put on the gaping hole inside of her, and giving in to them would only make her feel even more stupid.

She'd known better, damn it. Had known that it was a bad idea to open herself up to Matt. Why had she thought he would want her, when no one else had? Why had she thought he would have faith in her after everything she'd done to him?

She loaded the suitcases in the car, locked up the house and drove away on autopilot, unsure of where she wanted to go. All she knew was that she wanted to put as much distance between Matt's house and herself as she could manage and still be in Austin.

It was ridiculous, really, to be this upset. After all, she'd brought it on herself. She was the one who had walked out on him. She was the one who had told him over and over again that she had no staying power. So how could she blame him simply because he'd chosen to believe her? To believe the evidence?

Because she'd wanted him to be different, had wanted him to see past her defenses to the woman she kept under wraps. Sure, she'd been unlovable her whole life. Certainly, she'd never let anyone close enough to see inside her before. Of course, there was something wrong with her. Something defective that warned anyone who might care about her that she wasn't worth the effort.

She just wished she knew what it was. She'd rip it out, destroy it. Try to start over before the baby got here and realized just how unlucky it had been in the motherhood lottery.

She drove around for a while, got lost twice despite the fact that she had slowly learned the city over the past couple of months. But her concentration was shot and she found herself taking wrong turn after wrong turn.

She finally ended up in a hotel near the Arboretum, where every suite had an efficiency kitchen. It wasn't a perfect solution to her problem, by any means, but it would buy her some time as she figured out what to do.

Without Matt, she had no real reason to stay in Austin, and a part of her wanted to take the baby and run as soon as she could.

She knew thinking like that wasn't fair to Matt, but she wasn't in a particularly equitable mood at the moment. Did she understand why Matt had done what he did? Absolutely. Did she think he had a right to feel the way he did about her? No doubt. Was she angry as hell at him despite her understanding? Damn straight she was.

She'd taken a chance on him. She'd let him in. She'd trusted him when she didn't trust anybody and he had thrown that trust back in her face—after making love to her every way a man could love a woman. That was the part she didn't understand, the part she couldn't forgive. At least not yet. If he was going to toss her out on her ear, why had he made love to her first?

For revenge? To humiliate her? To hurt her? If so, he'd accomplished all three—and then some. It would be a long time before she forgot the lesson Matt had taught her today—if she ever did. And it would be longer still before she let anyone else get a chance at her heart.

It turned out that she'd been right all along—the lesson she'd learned when she was still a girl was actually dead-on. Love was a sucker's game, and in the end, the last one standing was the winner.

To hell with Matt and to hell with whatever she had hoped to build with him. When the dust had settled and everything had been cleared away, *she* would be the one still standing.

BY THE TIME MATT GOT HOME that evening, he was suffering from a headache so intense he could barely see. All day he'd been going over his last conversation with Camille and feeling guilty as hell over the way he'd handled it. Sure, he'd thought a quick break was better, had figured telling her right away—before either of them got in too deep—was the way to go. But the sad fact was, he had been in too deep from the night he'd opened his front door to find her standing, beautiful and pregnant, on his doorstep.

Blinded by the headache, he was in the house and calling Camille's name before he clued in that her silly yellow car had been missing from the driveway. He was running before the knowledge had fully sunk in, checking out her room and her studio, only to find them both empty. Nothing remained of her—not a gum wrapper in the wastebasket or a paintbrush in the sink. It was as if the four months she'd spent living in his house had never existed.

He hadn't expected her to leave this soon, had figured it would take her a few days—or weeks—to find a decent place to live. It hadn't occurred to him that she would just take her stuff and run, though looking back, he couldn't imagine what else she might have done. Stuck around, until an awkward situation became downright untenable? Yeah, right. Why should she stick it out when it was so much easier to pack a suitcase and run—like she always did? The only surprising thing about her behavior was that she had taken the time to gather all of her things before fleeing.

He wanted to rage about her running out without so much as a word or a forwarding address, but he'd never be able to look himself in the mirror again. He had driven Camille to this, had upset the delicate truce that they had arrived at by confusing sex and love. Again.

He was the one who had pushed her into this corner and now he was the one pissed off because she had come out swinging. He never would have guessed he was such a damn hypocrite.

Disgusted with Camille, with himself and with life in general, he prowled around the house, shocked at how empty it felt without her here. He'd thought it was bad those two days she was in New Orleans, but at least then he'd been able to head into her studio and look at her art. He'd studied her paintings and seen Camille's unique, vibrant take on the world.

Now even that was gone and all he was left with was himself. And he was lousy company.

A hard knock on his door pulled him out of his reverie, had him racing to the door with only one thought in his mind—that Camille had come back. About halfway down the stairs he realized just how ridiculous that supposition was, but he didn't turn back. He had a compulsive need to know, one way or the other, if she'd changed her mind.

Not that it would do him any good, because he hadn't changed his. Sure, he regretted the scene that had happened that morning between them, but that didn't mean he thought things could work out between them. They couldn't.

Pulling open the door, he braced himself for whatever he would find on his front porch. But nothing had prepared him for the sight of Reece there, a six-pack of beer in one hand and a bottle of Lagavulin in the other.

"What the hell are you doing here?" he demanded, too ornery to worry about being polite.

"Planning on getting rip-roaring drunk. You want to ask me in?"

Matt grunted, but moved aside to let the man in. "What have you got to get drunk about? I thought things were almost perfect over at the Sandler house."

The moment he said the words he regretted them— they made him sound jealous and bitter, when the truth was he didn't begrudge his friend one iota of the happiness he had. He'd walked through fire to get it.

Thankfully, Reece didn't take offense, just made a beeline for the bar and a couple of glasses. "They are. But things in the architectural office of Jenkins and Sandler aren't doing so hot."

"What do you mean?" A totally different type of alarm coursed through him. If the business was in trouble, how was he going to support Camille and the baby? "Is something wrong with the firm?"

"Something is wrong with you, my friend." Reece handed him a glass filled to the brim with two-hundred-dollar Scotch. "Now drink up and tell me what the hell happened between you and Camille."

"How do you know anything happened between us?" Matt countered, even as he took a healthy sip of his drink.

Reece snorted. "You were an absolute disaster today—on all fronts. Even the interns noticed. So if it isn't Camille, it had better be a terminal disease. Because nothing else gives you a pass for acting like a cross between the Grinch and Attila the Hun."

"She moved out."

"Whoa, seriously?" Reece straightened up, suddenly looking like he was taking this whole thing much more seriously. "She ran?"

"Not exactly."

"Well then, what? Because I know you weren't stupid enough to ask her to leave."

Matt winced before he could stop himself and Reece's eyes grew huge. "Are you shitting me? You kicked the mother of your child out of your house?"

"It's not the way you're making it sound."

"Really?" Reece arranged himself on the sofa, took a healthy swallow of his own drink. "Well then, spill it. Because I have got to hear how it was."

Matt spent the next few minutes pouring out the whole sordid story, and feeling worse for the retelling. Reece didn't make things any better when he muttered, "You're an asshole," before Matt was even halfway done with his recitation.

When he finally did finish, Reece was quiet so long that Matt began to wonder if his friend had fallen asleep with his eyes open. But there was no such luck.

"You know I mean this in the best possible way, man, but you screwed up. Big-time. You need to fix this."

"*I* need to fix it? She's the one who ducks and runs at the first sign of trouble."

"You told her to get out of your house after sleeping with her? And you thought she'd stick around? Knowing beforehand that the woman already has commitment issues?"

"Exactly. She's the one with commitment issues. It never would have worked out between us. I was just trying to save things before they got bad between us."

"And how's that working out for you?"

Matt shook his head in disgust. "Are you here to talk me to death or are you going to pour me another drink?"

"Both."

"Could we skip the first and keep the second coming?"

"Not on your life." But Reece poured him a second Scotch. Though this one was quite a bit smaller than the first, Matt figured it was prudent not to complain.

"So, what makes you think things are going to go bad?" Reece demanded. "Besides your incredibly well-developed sixth sense, of course."

"You're being a real smart-ass tonight, you know that?"

"You know what they say, Better a smart-ass…"

"Than a dumb ass." Matt finished the quote for him.

"Exactly. But seriously, why are you so sure things won't work between you two?"

"Come on, Reece. You've met her. You even said it yourself. She's got serious commitment issues."

"Yeah, but you're forgetting the most important question— Why does she have those issues?"

"Because she's a flake? Because she's an artist? Because she wants to see the whole damn world by the time she's thirty-five? How the hell should I know why she's so afraid to be in a relationship?"

"And it never occurred to you that that was where you should start?"

"Meaning?"

"Meaning, what's her family like?"

"Both her parents are dead, and I get the impression they were never close. She left home at seventeen."

"What about siblings?"

"She's an only child."

"Her best friend? What's she like?"

"I don't think she has one. Or at least she never mentions anyone."

Even as he said the words, he was beginning to feel like a total idiot. Why hadn't he seen this before? Why had he needed Reece to point it out to him?

"She doesn't know what it means to have a relationship with another person. That's what you're getting at, isn't it?"

Reece shrugged. "You would know that better than I do. But any woman who reaches the ripe old age of thirty-two without any entanglements—including close friends—must have a very good reason as to why that's true. Look at me. Because of what my dad put me through growing up, I was so afraid of failure that I almost let Sarah slip right through my fingers."

"That's different."

"Only because you know the circumstances. Might I suggest you find out Camille's circumstances before you make any judgment calls?"

"So what—you're saying I should have let things go on as they were for a while? Even after what she did to me?"

"What did she do to you, Matt? Besides walking out six months ago—per your original arrogance—what has she done that's so bad?"

"She took off for New Orleans."

"While you were halfway around the world. I'm not sure how that really affects you—especially since you left her first that time."

"Hey. Whose side are you on?"

Reece poured him another couple of fingers of Scotch. "Yours. Which is why I can't sit by and watch you screw this up for no reason."

"I have a reason. She all but admitted she was going to walk out again."

Reece paused right in the middle of his sanctimonious act. "She really said that?"

"Close enough. She said she wasn't stuck, that she could walk out whenever she wanted."

"But did she say she *wanted* to walk out?"

"Does it matter? If she hadn't walked out today, she would have sometime soon. I'd have spent the next weeks, months—the rest of my life—waiting for the other shoe to drop. I can't do that."

"So instead, you'll spend the rest of your life miserable and wanting to be with her? I'm not so sure that's a better bet, man."

Matt stood up abruptly, a little unsteady after three drinks, but still sober enough to see Camille's face as she told him she loved him. She'd looked frightened, yes, and vaguely ill, as she said the words—so ill, in fact, that he'd been unable to take them seriously.

But what if Reece was right—what if she'd never had the chance to be close to someone before? What if she'd cut him off at the knees all those months ago as a defense mechanism?

The cynical side of his nature told him he was being an idiot, that he was searching for an excuse where there wasn't any. But she'd looked so devastated when he'd told her he didn't want to be with her. As if her entire world had just gotten blown to pieces.

Which was exactly how he felt, no matter how many times he told himself this was for the best.

"I need to see her." He said the words quietly, then reached for the bottle of Scotch. If he was going to do this, he needed all the liquid courage he could get.

"That's the spirit." Reece yanked the bottle neatly out of his grasp. "I think you've had enough. No woman likes a stumbling-down drunk."

"Right. Absolutely." He was going to have to do this without the liquor, face rejection on his own.

Then an awful thought occurred to him, one so terrible that he actually had to sit down to keep his rubbery legs from going out from under him.

"What's wrong?" Reece demanded.

"I have no idea where to find her."

"Call her."

He snorted. "You don't know Camille. Hell will freeze over before she answers a call from me."

"Well, then, call…"

It was then that he realized just how alone Camille was in the world. If she'd wanted to find him, she could check with his family, his job, his friends. For her, there was no one to ask. He was the only one she'd trusted enough to let him inside of her and he'd turned around and knocked her on her ass.

"How many hotels are there in Austin?" he asked Reece grimly.

"I think we're about to find out."

CHAPTER SEVENTEEN

TWO WEEKS LATER, MATT PACED nervously in front of Rick's office as he waited for Camille. Between the two of them, he and Reece had called every hotel in Austin—at least twice—over the past thirteen days, but had never been able to find her. He'd been destroyed, on the brink of giving up, when he'd remembered about the ultrasound. Camille would be here, today, for her doctor's appointment, and he wasn't going to let her leave before he'd said his piece.

He'd tried calling her—four times a day. In his messages he'd apologized, begged for her to talk to him, even groveled, but she'd never called him back.

Which is why there was a healthy dose of anger—and fear—simmering along with his desperation to see her. He knew, only too well, that if Camille decided to write him out of her life, there was very little he could do about it.

Please, God, don't let her have given up on him completely.

Glancing at his watch for the fifth time in as many minutes, he saw the second hand had swept around the dial one more time. Her appointment was in ten minutes—if she didn't get here soon, there'd be no time for them to talk before they went up to Rick's office. And call him old-fashioned or superstitious or any of the other words, but he didn't want to find out the sex of his baby while he was feuding with its mother. It seemed like a bad omen.

Not that there was anything logical about such a feeling, but somewhere in the past two weeks, logic and order had gone out the window. He was going with desperation now.

He was just about to give up, to head to Rick's office and see if maybe she'd canceled, when he saw her hurrying across the parking lot. She was dressed in a long, violet maternity dress, one that hugged all of her new, mouthwatering curves, and his fingers literally itched to touch her.

Her wild hair was tumbling in its usual crazy curls down her back and huge gold hoops dangled from her ears. As she got closer, he realized her lips were slicked a sexy, powerful red and her cheeks were flushed a becoming rose. She looked healthy and happy and well-rested, as if she hadn't suffered one moment from being away from him. His heart sunk as he realized he might really have blown it—she might have already moved on and he had only himself to blame.

CAMILLE'S HEART SKIPPED a beat as she saw Reece waiting at the door of Rick's building. After all of the times he'd called her cell, she'd figured he would show up here and had dressed carefully for the meeting—she absolutely refused to let him see how badly he'd hurt her. Besides, confronting him here was better than doing it at his house, or at the apartment she'd moved into the week before. Neutral territory and all that, though she couldn't help wishing for home-court advantage as she watched him watch her.

"Showtime," she murmured to herself, then breezed up to the only man she'd ever loved.

"Matt," she said with a quick smile. "How are you?" She stood on her tiptoes to drop a kiss on his cheek—just to show him how little she was affected by him—and nearly blew the whole thing. He still smelled like the ocean, clean and fresh and so delicious that a part of her wanted to throw herself into his arms and say to hell with her pride. But he'd already rejected her once—in no uncertain terms—and she just didn't have it in her to put herself out there again.

Not like that.

As she took a step back, got her first real look at him, she was shocked at how disheveled he was. His normally pristine appearance was definitely the worse for wear—his shirt was buttoned wrong, he'd forgotten his belt and his hair was sticking up in twenty different directions, as if he hadn't been able to stop himself from trying to pull it out by the roots.

"Camille." His voice was hoarse, and it shot sparks right through her.

"Come on, Matt. Let's go inside." She headed up to the door. "We're going to be late."

"I don't care."

She froze in her tracks, turned around to stare at him in confusion. Since when did Matt not care about a schedule? About an appointment?

"Excuse me?"

"I need to talk to you, Camille."

"Can't it wait?" She really didn't think she could take any more from him, and had no desire to see the doctor with her heart on her sleeve.

"No. It can't wait. It's been waiting for two damn weeks. How could you just disappear like that?"

"Matt." She glanced around nervously. "People are starting to look."

"Do you think I care? I called you fifty-two times and you didn't answer one of my calls. How can a man say he's sorry, that he's made the biggest mistake of his life, if you won't even pick up the damn phone?" he raged.

"What did you say?"

"I said I love you, Camille. I've loved you for six long months and I'm sorry that I hurt you before. I was scared, terrified that you would leave me again. That you would get tired of me in a few months or a few years, that you would take the baby and leave me. And then where would I be? If I love you this much now, how much worse off would I be a year from now? Two?"

Camille felt as if she'd tumbled down the rabbit hole for the second time in as many months. "You love me."

"Of course I love you! Do you think I would have sent you away if I didn't? That I would have made such a god-awful, abysmal mess of our whole relationship if I wasn't scared stupid with it?"

Her heart trembled with the beginnings of joy. "You didn't make the mess on your own, you know. I helped... a little."

"Please, Camille, don't leave me again." His eyes burned almost black as he cupped her face in his big, warm hands. "Please don't let me have messed this up beyond repair."

"You really hurt me, Reece. But—"

"I'm sorry. God, I'm so sorry."

"Let me finish." She laid a hand on his chest, felt the steady beat of his heart beneath her palm and knew she'd found a steadfast man. Which was a good thing, because if there was one thing she had learned recently, it was that, all appearances to the contrary, she was a steadfast woman.

"But I hurt you, too," she continued. "And I'm sorry about that. More sorry than I can ever say."

"It doesn't matter. I just want—"

"Of course it matters. If I hadn't been so stubborn to begin with, we wouldn't have ended up in this predicament. But I want you to know that I came home from New Orleans with the understanding that you were it for me. I didn't know if we could make it work, if I could trust you—or myself—enough to stick around, but I knew I'd never feel about another man the way I feel about you.

"I've spent the past two weeks doing nothing but thinking about all the ways I've screwed this up, all the ways I'd pushed you away, and hurt you, because I couldn't trust that you would actually want me. That you could love me, when no one ever has before. But those are my insecurities, not yours. My faults, not yours." She reached for his hand, placed it on the growing curve of her stomach. "I want to marry you, Matt. I want to have your baby and build a life with you, starting right here, right now."

The color drained from his face and for a moment she was afraid she had made a terrible mistake. But then a smile split his face, so big and beautiful that she couldn't mistake it for anything else.

"Are you asking me to marry you, Camille?"

"Well, I figure it's my turn. You came here and groveled, told me you loved me when you expected me to shrug you off. It's only fair that I do this."

He cocked a disbelieving brow. "Well, aren't you a romantic?"

"This is me—you had to know I'd screw it up." She laughed, then laid a trembling hand over his.

"I love you, Matt Jenkins, and I want to spend the rest of my life showing you how much. Please, marry me, build a family with me. And, from time to time, when life gets to be too much, run away with me to someplace fabulous. Can you do that for me?"

Tears filled his eyes as he pulled her into his arms. "It would be my very great honor to marry you, Camille Arraby. I want nothing more than to make a life with you, and our child. And there're a million places I still want to see in this world—I'd like nothing more than to see them with you."

As he leaned down and took her mouth with his own, Camille knew this wasn't the end of life as she knew it. It was only the beginning. A beautiful, amazing, wonderful beginning.

And when, minutes later, she and Matt watched their son twist and squirm his way across the ultrasound screen, Camille realized that she couldn't wait for the next chapter in their grand adventure to start. Reaching over, she squeezed Matt's hand, and as he smiled at her, she understood that he felt exactly the same way.

* * * * *

COMING NEXT MONTH

Available August 10, 2010

LARGER-PRINT BOOKS!
GET 2 FREE LARGER-PRINT NOVELS PLUS
2 FREE GIFTS!

HARLEQUIN®

Super Romance®

Exciting, emotional, unexpected!

YES! Please send me 2 FREE LARGER-PRINT Harlequin® Superromance® novels and my 2 FREE gifts (gifts are worth about $10). After receiving them, if I don't wish to receive any more books, I can return the shipping statement marked "cancel." If I don't cancel, I will receive 6 brand-new novels every month and be billed just $5.44 per book in the U.S. or $5.99 per book in Canada. That's a saving of at least 13% off the cover price! It's quite a bargain! Shipping and handling is just 50¢ per book.* I understand that accepting the 2 free books and gifts places me under no obligation to buy anything. I can always return a shipment and cancel at any time. Even if I never buy another book from Harlequin, the two free books and gifts are mine to keep forever.

139/339 HDN E5PS

Name _____ (PLEASE PRINT) _____

Address _____ Apt. # _____

City _____ State/Prov. _____ Zip/Postal Code _____

Signature (if under 18, a parent or guardian must sign) _____

Mail to the **Harlequin Reader Service:**
IN U.S.A.: P.O. Box 1867, Buffalo, NY 14240-1867
IN CANADA: P.O. Box 609, Fort Erie, Ontario L2A 5X3
Not valid for current subscribers to Harlequin Superromance Larger-Print books.

Are you a current subscriber to Harlequin Superromance books and want to receive the larger-print edition? Call 1-800-873-8635 today!

* Terms and prices subject to change without notice. Prices do not include applicable taxes. N.Y. residents add applicable sales tax. Canadian residents will be charged applicable provincial taxes and GST. Offer not valid in Quebec. This offer is limited to one order per household. All orders subject to approval. Credit or debit balances in a customer's account(s) may be offset by any other outstanding balance owed by or to the customer. Please allow 4 to 6 weeks for delivery. Offer available while quantities last.

Your Privacy: Harlequin Books is committed to protecting your privacy. Our Privacy Policy is available online at www.eHarlequin.com or upon request from the Reader Service. From time to time we make our lists of customers available to reputable third parties who may have a product or service of interest to you. If you would prefer we not share your name and address, please check here. ☐

Help us get it right—We strive for accurate, respectful and relevant communications. To clarify or modify your communication preferences, visit us at www.ReaderService.com/consumerschoice.

HSRLP10R

*Five hunky Texas single fathers—five stories from
Cathy Gillen Thacker's* LONE STAR DADS *miniseries.
Here's an excerpt from the latest,* THE MOMMY PROPOSAL
from Harlequin American Romance.

"I hear you work miracles," Nate Hutchinson drawled.
Brooke Mitchell had just stepped into his lavishly appointed
office in downtown Fort Worth, Texas.

"Sometimes, I do." Brooke smiled and took the sexy
financier's hand in hers, shook it briefly.

"Good." Nate looked her straight in the eye. "Because
I'm in need of a home makeover—fast. The son of an old
friend is coming to live with me."

She was still tingling from the feel of his warm palm.
"Temporarily or permanently?"

"If all goes according to plan, I'll adopt Landry by
summer's end."

Brooke had heard the founder of Nate Hutchinson
Financial Services was eligible, wealthy and generous to a
fault. She hadn't known he was in the market for a family,
but she supposed she shouldn't be surprised. But Brooke
had figured a man as successful and handsome as Nate
would want one the old-fashioned way. *Not that this was
any of her business...*

"So what's the child like?" she asked crisply, trying not
to think how the marine-blue of Nate's dress shirt deepened
the hue of his eyes.

"I don't know." Nate took a seat behind his massive
antique mahogany desk. He relaxed against the smooth
leather of the chair. "I've never met him."

"Yet you've invited this kid to live with you permanently?"

"It's complicated. But I'm sure it's going to be fine."

Obviously Nate Hutchinson knew as little about teenage

boys as he did about decorating. But that wasn't her problem. Finding a way to do the assignment without getting the least bit emotionally involved was.

Find out how a young boy brings Nate and Brooke together in THE MOMMY PROPOSAL, coming August 2010 from Harlequin American Romance.